THE GIRL IN THE PARK

THE GIRL IN THE PARK
MARIAH FREDERICKS

schwartz & wade books · new york

Text copyright © 2012 by Mariah Fredericks
Jacket photograph of girl copyright © 2012 by Jason Todd/Rubberball/Getty Images; jacket photograph of Central Park © 2012 by Eileen O'Donnell/Flickr/Getty Images

Schwartz & Wade Books and the colophon are trademarks of Random House, Inc.

Grateful acknowledgment is made to Jon Landau Management for permission to reprint an excerpt from "Yesterday's Child" by Patti Scialfa, copyright © 2004 by Patti Scialfa (ASCAP). All rights reserved. International copyright secured. Reprinted by permission.

Visit us on the Web! randomhouse.com/kids

Educators and librarians, for a variety of teaching tools, visit us at randomhouse.com/teachers

Library of Congress Cataloging-in-Publication Data
Fredericks, Mariah.
The girl in the park / Mariah Fredericks.—1st ed.
p. cm.
Summary: When a teenaged girl with a bad reputation is murdered in New York City's Central Park after a party, her childhood friend is determined to solve the mystery of who caused her death.
ISBN 978-0-375-86843-6 (trade) — ISBN 978-0-375-96843-3 (glb) — ISBN 978-0-375-89907-2 (ebook)
[1. Mystery and detective stories.   2. Murder—Fiction.   3. High schools—Fiction.
4. Schools—Fiction.]
I. Title.
PZ7.F872295 Gi 2012
[Fic]—dc23
2011012309

The text of this book is set in 11.5-point Augustal.
Book design by Rachael Cole
Printed in the United States of America

10 9 8 7 6 5 4 3 2 1

First Edition

FOR THE ONES WHO NEVER
MADE IT HOME
AND THEIR FAMILIES

DAY ONE

In my dream, everyone talks except me. It's a party, and I'm surrounded by voices. I listen. I smile. I nod. No one is actually speaking to me. But still—I want to pretend I'm a part of it.

Faces spin by in a blur. More people now, and still more. They laugh, tease, point fingers. Their talk becomes a meteor shower of sound, the words coming too fast and hard to understand.

And maybe because I am silent, I'm the one who sees her. Wendy. She's standing in a wide-open window. The city stretches vast and dark behind her. Her toes are poised on the sill, her fingertips just reach the edges. There is nothing to hold her as she stares into the crowded room.

All of a sudden, she wobbles. Her fingers lose their hold. Now it's all balance. Her arms flail, a foot rises. I am too far away, I can't reach her in time.

Stop! I yell. But it comes out an ugly blurted *Op!* People glance over, embarrassed, go back to their talk.

She's falling! This is *She alling!* Someone giggles. Another girl tries to hide her smile.

Desperate, I scream, *Someone help her! Thomeone elper!*

Now the laughter starts. As everyone swings toward me,

pointing and snickering, Wendy falls, but no one sees. I howl, *No, no!* as I feel my heart fall with her.

And someone's knocking at the door.

I open my eyes, see my mom standing by my bed. Still dazed from the dream, I take in my purple quilt covered in stars, Sullivan the blue whale perched at the foot of my bed, the post-card mosaic on the opposite wall. Faces, because I like faces. Greta Garbo. Edith Piaf. Lucy from *Peanuts.*

I struggle up, croak, "Hey, Mom."

"Rain, honey, I'm sorry to wake you."

I look at the clock. 7:16. We're visiting my grandmother today, but even so, this is way, way early for Sunday morning. Particularly when I've been to a party the night before. Which my mother knows. So what gives?

Blinking, I say, "It's fine. What's up?"

"Ms. Geller's on the phone. She's looking for Wendy."

My mom looks at me. *What is this?*

I look back. *I have no idea.*

As we walk down the hall, my mom asks, "Was Wendy at the party last night?"

Wendy doesn't miss parties. "Yeah, she was there."

"I didn't know she was still a close friend."

I make a face like, *I didn't either.*

Now we're at the kitchen. I pick up the phone. "Hi, Ms. Geller."

"Rain? I'm so sorry to call this early." She's talking fast, a little too loud. *Scared,* I think, *but trying not to be.*

"No problem at all. What can I do?"

"Well . . ." Big sigh, ends on a shaky laugh. *Everything's okay!* "Wendy did not come home last night."

Faces start flashing in my head. Snatches of conversation. Wendy surrounded by people, laughing—she's always laughing.

I hear Ms. Geller say, "And, uh, I'm just hoping there's a very rational explanation." Again, the weird shaky laugh.

"Oh, absolutely," I say.

"You were at Karina Burroughs's party last night, right?"

"Yes. Wendy was there. I definitely saw her."

"Was she . . . How do I ask this? Was she okay?"

Wendy using two hands to lift a gallon of vodka, sloshing it over a line of plastic cups. *Party time!*

"Um, it was a party. But when I saw her, she was fine."

"When did you last see her? Can you remember?"

"I left early," I apologize. "Before midnight. So probably I saw her at . . ."

Hey, Nico . . .

"Eleven? Eleven-thirty?" I say.

"And she was okay?"

I make agony eyes at my mom, and she squeezes my hand.

"She had had some alcohol," I say carefully. "But she wasn't over the edge or anything."

"Anyone she was with? A boy?"

Come be with me, Nico.

I hate this. I don't want to tell this woman things she doesn't want to know. "She has lots of friends, Ms. Geller. Everybody likes Wendy."

Even as I say this, I wonder why I'm saying it. Because it's not true.

I finish lamely, "I'm sure she's fine."

"But there's no one you can remember she might have stayed with?"

"Did you try Karina? Or Jenny Zalgat?"

"Oh, yes." Ms. Geller's voice turns chilly. "They couldn't be bothered to come to the phone."

Hung over, I think. Or protecting Wendy. No—protecting themselves.

I hesitate. There is one other name I could give Ms. Geller.

I blurt out, "Nico Phelps. You could call him."

"Nico Phelps." A pause. She's writing it down. "You don't have his number?"

"No, I'm sorry."

"Okay." Deep breath. "Okay. Thank you. This is—"

"You truly don't need to thank me, Ms. Geller. I bet Wendy calls the second you hang up."

"Probably." She almost laughs this time, then says, "Actually, that's another thing."

"What?"

"I've tried calling her cell phone. There's no answer."

Wendy checking her cell, chucking it back in her bag. *Somebody's playing mommy again. As if she gives a crap.*

"Sounds like she's feeling a little defiant," I joke.

"I hope," says Ms. Geller. "I mean, that that's . . ."

She stops herself. "Anyway, sweetie, thank you. When this is over, I want you to come to dinner. We'd love to see you. It's been so long."

"Yeah, same. And—"

"Yes?"

"Let me know. When it all works out."

"I will." And she hangs up.

* * *

4

"Wendy Geller," says my mom, pouring us both coffee. "You haven't been friends with her in years."

"Not since ninth grade." I pour milk in, watch it bleed through the dark, clear coffee and turn it muddy. "Total besties until we realized, Hm, we actually have nothing in common."

My mom nods in her pretend wise woman way. "You were very different girls."

"Yeah. She was cool, though."

Cleft palate. Big deal. Okay, maybe you sound a little funny. Some. Times. But you need to forget about that and speak up, girl!

Wendy is dropping frozen cookie dough on a baking sheet. Turning, she says, "Because can I say something? Most people? Myself included? Talk way too much. You. On the other hand. Listen. *And* you think. So when you do speak? You're brilliant. So, give up the silence, okay?"

We are sitting in my kitchen at an old wooden table. My mom likes blue and white; you can see it in the white curtains, the blue tiles on the wall. A vase of sunflowers sits on the windowsill, big and ridiculously beautiful.

I tug on one of the petals. I am thrilled by Wendy's compliment and do not know what to say. My whole life, people have been telling me to speak, and it's just one more thing that's wrong with me. *Rain does not participate in class. Speak up, I can't understand you.* Years of speech therapy have helped my s's, sharpened my t's. But I still hate how I sound: mushmouthed and nasal. Even if people can understand me, why would they want to listen?

Wendy is the first person to tell me I might have something

to say. And she gives me this amazing present as if it's nothing. As if it's no big deal to tell someone, You're cool, you're normal. You don't have to hide.

A blob of dough in her hand, Wendy says, "And now I have a question—why are we baking these?"

Me laughing. "Not sure."

"The dough rocks raw, am I right?"

"You are so right."

"She was sweet," I tell my mom. "She had a good heart." Then I wonder: Why am I talking about this girl in the past? *Because you don't know her anymore,* comes the answer.

I say, "I don't know why her mom called me."

"Maybe because you're the last sane friend she had." My mom holds out the bagel basket.

Taking a poppyseed bagel, I say, "There are a few other sane people at my school, Mom."

My mom sings opera. Like for a living. She's not Renée Fleming, but if you're into opera, you probably know her. Maybe it's all that time she spends with Verdi and Mozart, but she has very high standards. One of the things she says: "If you eat junk and you watch junk, you turn into . . ." "Junk?" I guess. "Exactly." Luckily she also has a sense of humor and has been known to pig out on Chinese food and *Project Runway* marathons.

Even though Wendy and I haven't been friends for almost two years, sometimes I'll tell my mom things I've heard about her. Why, I'm not sure. Maybe it's hard to get my head around the fact that someone I was once friends with would be doing those things.

All of which is to say: my mom doesn't have the highest opinion of Wendy.

Now I say, "It's important to Wendy for people to like her."

"So she becomes the kind of person people 'like' instead of the person she really is."

"Ma . . ."

My mom reaches out and squeezes my hand. "I'm sorry. Just her poor mother was so scared and . . . thank you," she says suddenly. "For not doing that to me. If you're ever that mad at me, hit me with a frying pan."

"Really?" I grin at the thought.

"Well, maybe a pillow. But don't let it get to this point." My mom shudders, picks up her coffee. "Who's Nico Phelps? I haven't heard that name before."

"There's a reason for that." I look at the clock. "We should get ready for Grandma's."

"Ooh, gosh!" My mom leaps off the chair, her kimono flying.

Later, as we're heading toward the car, my mom says, "So, what's really going on here?" and I know she means Wendy.

I hold up my hands like, *Who knows?*

My grandma lives in Connecticut. Unless she has a performance, my mom visits her every Sunday. Every other Sunday, I come. And my mom, being my mom, insists on no iPods, and cell phones turned off. Because "when you're with a person, you should be with that person. Not distracted by five million other things."

But I can't help it. Today I'm distracted. Not by five million things, just one. Wendy.

Last night, on my way to the party, I wondered, Okay, what will Wendy do tonight?

Will she get bombed? Probably yes.

Say something outrageous? Pretty sure yep.

Take off all or most of her clothes? Always a chance.

Kiss, grope, or whatever, someone? Likelihood strong.

Chance that that someone will be someone else's boyfriend? 99.9 %.

Then I thought about the particularly insane thing she had promised to do that night. And I wondered two things: Doesn't she know how ridiculous she is? And what is that like? To have no fear?

My mom taps me on the leg. "We're here."

My grandmother lives in Litchfield, in a house some people would call a mansion but she would insist is just a house. My mom grew up here. She rode horses. It looks like the kind of place you ride horses. Lots of grass. Lots of quiet. White houses and American flags. It's one of those drizzly, cold November days; when we arrive, my mom and I hurry from the car to the door.

It used to be when we visited my grandmother, she'd open the door herself, fold first me, then my mom in a big hug. "Glory be, you're here!" Now the nurse answers the door with a big smile and calls, "Ms. Donovan, look who's come to lunch!" Of course, my grandmother can't look because she's in the living room. In a wheelchair.

So my mom takes off her coat and asks the nurse, whose name is Gwen, how my mom is. Which means, Tell me what to expect. And Gwen murmurs, She's fine, doing fine. Which means, No change. Meanwhile, I go down the hall, calling, "Grandma?"

Since her stroke, my grandmother can't move her right side. As I come through the door, I see her sitting in her chair, staring out at the garden, as if something she wants is out there but she's not sure how to get it. I hesitate, confused by her distance. But then she seems to recognize that I'm here. Her left hand rises and her blue eyes brighten.

Hugging her, I say, "Hey, Grandma, you look great."

She peers at me. ". . . oo ook ike . . . oo." *You look like you.*

"And that's okay?" My hands go to the chopsticks in my hair. Most people make me feel self-conscious, but only two people have the right to: my mother and my grandmother.

"Gr-r-rand."

My mom comes running in like she's a teenager and her mom is her best friend who she hasn't seen in forever. She gives her a big, long hug, then whispers, "Guess what I brought." My grandmother shakes her head. *"Cheesecake."*

Over lunch, which still takes place in the formal dining room at a table meant for twelve, my grandmother asks, "'ow's sool?"

I catch a flash of anxiety from my mom; she has a hard time understanding my grandmother these days. "School's hard," I say, translating for her.

"Junior year is so much pressure," says my mom.

My grandmother makes a face. ". . . 'oo serious. Have fun."

"I have fun," I assure her.

"Just last night, she went to a party," my mother chimes in. My grandmother raises her eyebrow: *And what did you get up to?*

"Nothing, Grandma. You know me."

Can I make a suggestion?

Wendy transferred to our school in ninth grade. Right away,

9

it was clear she didn't belong. First off, she was from Long Island. Her parents had split up a year earlier, and her mom had just moved back to the city. Rich city and rich suburbia are not the same. It showed in Wendy's clothes, in her hair. You heard it in her voice. B&T, people sniffed. Bridge and Tunnel. And the fact that she wanted so bad to fit in just made it worse.

At our school, everybody is the child of a Somebody. That kid's dad is a real estate mogul, that kid's mom is a judge, that one's uncle wrote the script for *Batman*. Wendy's mom and dad were no one you'd heard of. Her grandparents were paying the bills for Alcott, and their money was something tacky like pool cleaner. For a while, Wendy had the nickname Pond Scum.

In ninth grade, I was feeling like I didn't belong, either. My two best friends had left—one moved to Westchester, the other transferred. They'd been my islands of safety, people I could float to in class or the cafeteria. They never made fun of how I talked, and because of them, I rarely had to talk to people who might. Now I was starting high school lost in a sea of people who thought I sounded like the Elephant Man.

Not that they said so to my face. Anymore. Sure, some kids still wiggled their fingers in fake sign language at me in the hallway. ("Sounds so weird, she must be deaf," ha, ha.) But most of it was more subtle. Like the first week of school when I had to ask Nora Acheson how many chapters to read for History of the Renaissance. She frowned as I talked, her mouth tight with embarrassment. Then once I'd ground to a halt, she said in a resentful voice, "I'm sorry, I did not understand that. *What* did you say?"

I knew my mistake. I had dared to speak. The rule at Alcott was simple: if you are not okay, keep it to yourself. Do not inflict yourself on those better than you. Stay silent. Keep your head down. Leave us alone—and we'll leave you alone. Remind us of the depressing fact that you exist and we will punish you however we see fit.

Which was why what Wendy did that day in the hallway was so completely and utterly astonishing.

I had free study and I was headed to the library. As I walked down the hall, I noticed a girl standing smack-dab in the middle. I recognized her as the new girl, the one from Long Island with bad hair that nobody liked. She was pushy, was what people said. And I saw why. Every single person who passed, she yelled, "Hey there!" The more popular kids got a sad little body check and questions—"What's up for the weekend?" "Could you believe that assignment?"

I slowed down, wincing at every Hey and How you doing? She was so wrong it was scary, and most kids brushed her off without a second glance. But she didn't quit. I noticed that, too. It was horribly fascinating. Like watching someone pound nails into their skull, again and again, with a big crazy smile on their face.

Eventually the crowd thinned out and it was only us left. I stood there watching as Wendy paced back and forth. This girl was so out there. Even when she was alone, you could read every emotion. She moved her head from side to side, threw her hands in the air, folded her arms, unfolded them.

Then burst out with, "How am I such an *idiot*?"

I laughed. Because here I was thinking she was so different from me, so insanely confident. But she felt like an idiot the same way I did.

Impulsively, I said, "Can I make a suggestion?"

Now, this probably came out like "Shuh-gesh-on." T's and s's still kicked my ass. And there was a moment before Wendy spoke when we both realized she had a choice. If she was a wannabe, she'd make fun of me. Clamp up her nose and say, "Yush?"

But instead she laughed. At herself, not me.

"God, yes, please. Anything."

She was friendly. She was eager. She acted like I knew what I was talking about, so I acted that way too. "You're trying too hard," I told her. "And you're going after the wrong people. Girls like Honor and Rima—forget them. They're sophomores and they're popular. You need to aim for their third-level friend. The girls that hang with top girls, but secretly? Resent them. You can be the outside friend they complain to. Then once you're deemed okay? You work your way up."

She came to stand next to me. "So, who should I be talking to?"

I thought. "Try Karina Burroughs. Maybe Colby Breslin. Jenny Zalgat."

She took those names in, then asked, "How'd you figure this stuff out?"

"I've watched these people my whole life."

"But . . ." She hesitated. "What? You don't care if they like you?"

This had never occurred to me, that I could be the one to choose. That, rather than being rejected, I could just not care. "Kind of," I said, trying to look bored by it all.

"That's cool. I could never do it." She grinned. "But it's cool. Wendy, by the way."

"Rain."

*   *   *

". . . 'ow are your friends?" my grandmother asks. " 'aylor?"

Taylor. "Still writing for the paper," I say. "Still crazed."

I realize: Taylor stayed at the party after I left. I should have told Ms. Geller to call her. Except that Taylor would tell her the whole story, and I still wasn't sure that was a good idea.

My grandmother asks about my singing, which I hate talking about around my mom because she always pretends I'm better than I am. I'm not terrible. But I'm not her and I know it.

"B-oyfriends?" my grandmother wants to know.

"I'm off men," I tell her.

She leans in. ". . . Lucas?"

I roll my eyes. "Yeah—what did happen to Lucas, Grandma?"

"He was an actor," says my mom dismissively. "*That's* what happened to Lucas."

"Do you think he'd go out with me?"

I had to look twice to make sure I was seeing the right person. Cam Davies? Was Wendy serious? We'd been friends for a month, and already I knew, you couldn't always be sure.

Just in case, I shook my head. "Girlfriend."

"Is it serious?"

"Wendy." I looked at her.

She giggled. "I'm just asking."

Just then, two girls walked by. They were second-level girls, not to be spoken to. But Wendy smiled, gave them a big "Hi!"

She'd broken the rules and I braced myself, knowing what was coming. The girls stopped. And stared. Then one of them, Gillian Lasker, made a flushing sound—the new joke was toilet cleaner, not pools. Laughing wildly, they hurried down the hall.

I muttered, "Jerks."

Wendy didn't answer. She just kept staring down the hall at Cam Davies.

Later, the rain clears and we take a walk around the garden. It's beautiful with the fallen leaves and the smell of freshness in the air. My mom says to Grandma, "Give me a quarter and I'll move in."

From her wheelchair, Grandma waves her hand. *Forget it.* She hates having a nurse, hates being taken care of. A lot of her old friends she doesn't see anymore.

My mom says she's crazy. But I understand. My mom doesn't know what it's like to be less than perfect, how people zoom in on that until it's all they see. Maybe because it weirds them out . . . or maybe because it makes them feel better about themselves.

People do pretty ugly things to make themselves feel better, this I do know.

"I jerked him off."

The first party we went to together, Wendy slept over at my house afterward. When she said that, I leaned out of my bed to look at her. But I couldn't see her face in the dark.

"Who and what are you talking about?" I asked, really, really hoping she'd say, *Just kidding. God.*

But she said, "Daniel. At the party."

Then she laughed. "It shot straight across the bathroom. I left it on the towels."

"That'll thrill Evie's parents." Because I still thought about parents with these things.

"Oh, Evie's a bitch, who cares?" She yawned.

Then I thought of something else: Gillian Lasker in the hall-way. "Doesn't Daniel have a girlfriend?"

There was a silence. Then Wendy said, "She should know to say hi when someone says hi to her."

"'at goes," my grandmother says, pointing to a dead bush.

"Tell the gardener," agrees my mom. Walking up to the bush, she touches the dry, leafless branches. They snap right off, get tangled in the rest. It looks like a nest of bones.

"This was so pretty," says my mom. "I wonder what hap-pened."

What happened? I think. That's always what you ask. What happened with Lucas? What happened with Wendy?

She's with Nico, I tell myself. And it's a big drama and she's the star. If she goes home, she turns back into plain old Wendy Geller, pool cleaner princess.

"I hate my mother."

Wendy glared around her living room. "Look at this place. She gets everything wrong. But hey, she lives at the office, what does she care?"

For the first few months we were friends, I didn't see Wendy's apartment. We always went to my place. Finally, one Saturday after a movie, she said, "Come see the hellhole."

Wendy lived in the East Seventies. "Fancy address, crap place," she told me. It wasn't a hellhole, but it was very different from my rambling, color-mad apartment, where you couldn't walk without tripping over books, CDs, or carpet fringe. The walls in Wendy's place were white plaster. No curtains, just blinds. The couches and chairs were beige and oatmeal, the tables glass. There was one shelf of books, mostly self-help and dieting. The kitchen was bare, except for one plastic bowl with some dried-up lemons. The place was quiet, but empty quiet rather than peaceful quiet. A motel you stayed in for one night before getting where you needed to be.

We went to Wendy's room. The furniture here was mostly IKEA, but she'd gotten a few bright funky things—a pillow shaped like a strawberry, a polka-dot lampshade. She'd covered the plaster walls with magazine cutouts. Glistening male bodies and girls with lots of hair and angry eyes. Flopping on her bed, Wendy said, "I should just go live with my dad. Of course, he now has Heidi, who I totally can't stand. Uck—you're so lucky having a cool family."

I thought about my mom and grandmother. Also, about the dad whose name I knew but I'd never met. About the half brother who didn't know I existed. About his mother, my dad's wife. Was that cool? It was complicated. But I didn't think Wendy was interested in that.

Rolling onto her stomach, Wendy said, "So—guess who I talked to today?"

"Who?"

"Seth. Cu-ute Seth with the shoulders."

I nodded, even as I thought of Seth's girlfriend Rima Nolan, one of those top girls who still thought Wendy was trash.

Wendy stared at me; she wanted more. Was I supposed to say, Yeah, cool? Bring up Rima? What?

Sometimes, when I didn't know what to say to Wendy, I talked to her in my head. Now I thought, Well, gee, first you went after Cam Davies. Then it was Daniel Ettinger. Last weekend, Malcolm Liddell. You're not with any of them now. Their girlfriends—or ex-girlfriends—hate you. Every girl in school worries you'll go after her guy.

"I didn't know you were into Seth," I said lamely.

She grinned. "Ab-so-loot-ly."

Really? I thought. *Because, maybe I'm crazy, but I never heard you talk about Seth until Rima gave you the stink eye when you complimented her skirt in the cafeteria.*

"Seth's going to Jenny's party this weekend." Wendy rolled over on her side. "I can tell my mom I'm with you, right?"

"Right." I had stopped going to parties with Wendy after the thing with Daniel and the towels. But Wendy still told her mom she was with me whenever she wanted to go out.

"Maybe you could come this time," Wendy said casually.

Immediately, I shook my head.

"It's just a *party*," she said, joking, but annoyed also. "It won't kill you to go."

It might, I thought. A lot of times, when I had to speak to someone, my heart pounded so bad I was convinced it was going to explode. And I didn't know how to tell Wendy she was different at parties. Someone not my friend, almost like the girls who made fun of me.

She shrugged. "I mean, unless you're going to be some kind of virgin nun your whole life . . ."

I stared, but Wendy's face was blank, as if she hadn't said the ugly thing she'd just said. I knew very well that speaking and the other thing went together. If you never talked to people, the chances of getting someone interested in you were pretty much zilch. And it was more than that. Guys took courage. Out-thereness. Sharing your thoughts, souls, bodies. Whatever—I was too scared for all of it.

I had thought that was my secret. Now Wendy, my supposed best friend, was calling me on it.

Maybe to prove I did have the guts to speak, I snapped, "Well, better a virgin nun than the opposite."

I don't know who was more shocked, me or Wendy. She immediately sat up and pulled her legs up to her chin. Wrapping her arms around them, she put her head down, face turned away from me.

I felt awful. Also thrilled. *Yeah, I can be nasty too.* Because that was another secret. The hope that one day, someone would push me too hard and I'd say something so scorchingly cruel that no one would ever mess with me again.

Take it back, Rain, I thought. Unsay what you said. The whole world hurts Wendy. Yay, you; you can do it, too.

"Wen?"

She wouldn't look at me.

"I'm sorry. I totally suck, that was . . . wrong."

There was a long silence. Then, her head still turned, she mumbled, "I suck too."

"Me, more."

She looked up, grinning. "No way. I so outrank you in suckage."

Laughing, I said, "Okay, you win."

"Which means you have to come to the party," she said triumphantly. "I will totally stick by you the whole time, I promise."

Then she added, "Seriously, dude. Those people are harsh. I need one person there that I know is on my side."

An island of safety.

How could I say no?

"How's Katherine Palmer?" my mom asks. She's going through my grandmother's friends one by one. At each name, my grandmother just shakes her head. I sit in the middle, wishing this would end.

"Call her," says my mom after every shake of the head. "Invite her over."

My grandmother glares, but it doesn't stop my mom. "You need your friends," she insists. "They need you."

"Things . . . change," says my grandmother.

Five minutes after we arrived at the party, Wendy dumped me cold, and I was living my worst nightmare: silent and lost in a roomful of people. I smiled, nodded, pretended to be one of the group. I watched Wendy work her way over to Seth, listened as she giggled and shrieked, *Oh my God, that's hilarious.*

I prayed for her to stop, prayed for her to come back, to be my friend again. If I was her home base, shouldn't she be mine? Wendy had said these people were harsh, and they were. Harsh and shallow and only into themselves. And Wendy seemed to get along with them just fine.

Who are you? I wondered. And why did I ever think we were friends?

When Wendy and Seth disappeared into the bedroom, I left and wandered in the hallway of Jenny's building. Wendy and I were supposed to go home together; I couldn't split. But I couldn't stay in there. Sitting on the cold, white marble steps, I decided I had been exiled to some barren Arctic wilderness. All around me there was snow, ice, frigid winds. No sign of human life anywhere.

Then Rima Nolan ran out into the hallway.

I heard her before I saw her: the ragged crying, the sharp echo of heels on the tiled floor. I felt a flutter of heat and movement as she rushed past me and up the stairs. I don't think she saw me at all.

The crying continued, growing faint as she climbed. I glanced down the hall, thinking Rima's friends would follow. But no one came.

Not right, I found myself thinking. *Come on, people, girl's in pain. You can't just leave her.*

But they could, it seemed.

The silence and emptiness of the hallway began to frighten me. Gazing up the stairs, I listened for Rima. Heard nothing.

Raising my voice slightly, I said, "Um, are you all right?"

No answer. I noticed that the hallway windows were open. This was a twelve-story building. We were on the ninth floor; the street lay far below us. And Rima was headed up. Last year at a party, Nellie Callender got massively drunk and tried to jump out a window.

Standing, I called up the stairs, "Hey!" Cringing as it echoed through the stairwell.

All I got back was silence.

Nervous, I climbed to the next floor. Then the next, until I heard the crying again, that ugly whining noise of real pain. I reached the top floor to find Rima wiping her nose with her sleeve. Bone thin with straight dark hair and enormous gray eyes, Rima was something out of Brontë, which I'd always frantically envied.

I kept my distance. Rima had never been mean to me, but I'd stayed out of her way, so she'd never had the chance. Now I was breaking the Thou Shalt Not Speak rule. And I was Wendy's friend. She would have every right to blast me.

Then Rima whispered, "They're laughing."

"What?" I came closer.

"Laughing." Her voice was stronger now. "Everyone. They're hanging out by the bedroom door, listening. They think it's hysterical."

I felt sick. Rima, I realized, had always thought those kids were nice because they were nice to her. Now she was seeing how ugly some of them could be. Welcome to the other side, I thought.

"I think . . . I think they're pretty drunk," I said softly, not sure if I meant her friends or Seth and Wendy.

"No excuse," she choked out.

"Nope," I agreed.

Rima looked up, as if she suddenly realized who she was talking to. I stepped back. "I'm probably the last person you want to talk to, I'm sorry. I'll go get . . ." I gestured downstairs, even as I wondered who I was going to get.

"No," said Rima more calmly. "It's cool. Hey, you came up here."

You. When Rima said that without contempt, the red burning hurt I'd felt, oh, it seemed like forever, cooled. In an instant, I wasn't the freak girl who talked funny or Wendy's coverfriend. I was just a person helping someone out.

Glancing toward the window, I said, "I have this very melodramatic mind. I was worried you were going to jump."

She grinned. "I'm scared of heights."

"Oh." And for no real reason, I laughed.

Rima laughed too. Then she stopped. "This kind of feels like falling," she said quietly. "All these people . . . you think they care about you. They'll be there for you. And then they . . ."

I thought of Wendy, how she promised she'd be with me at the party. "Then they let you fall."

"Yeah." But she laughed again.

"At least," I said, "after you fall, you land on solid ground. You know where you stand."

She smiled. "And what if you're smashed into a million pieces?"

"Yeah, that could be a problem."

She sat. After a moment, I sat too. The two of us on one little ledge of white marble step. She talked about Seth, about her friends. Her parents, what they expected of her. How she was just a little sick and tired of the whole thing.

I listened. And it seemed to help both of us.

The conversation about friends seems to tire my grandmother out. She grows quiet. Her gaze drifts back to the garden. I give my mom a look, and she nods. Standing, she says, "I so want to stay, but we have to go."

Gwen brings my grandmother to the door. As we walk down the long hallway, I check to make sure Grandma hasn't actually fallen asleep. But no, her eyes are open, focused on the long stretch of hallway that leads to the door.

As we put on our coats, Grandma hands me an envelope. Taking it, I can feel photographs inside. She says, "M-m-y m-o . . . ther. And sis . . ."

She struggles and I say, "Your sister?"

She nods. Recently, she's started doing this, giving me family photos. Images of people I don't know but I'm connected to in some strange way. I'm not sure why she doesn't give them to my mom, but my mom says, "Just take them. It gives her pleasure."

Then my grandmother says suddenly, "-endy!"

My mom and I look at each other. "Who, Grandma?" I ask.

Her mouth works. "W-endy . . ."

". . . Wendy."

We say it at the same time. My grandmother nods. "Wha happen . . . Wendy?"

What happened to Wendy? I hesitate. For some strange reason, I want to tell my grandmother, *I don't know. I don't know what happened to Wendy and . . .*

I'm scared. I don't know why that comes into my head. Wendy's partying in Atlantic City with Nico. She's fine. Or she's not with Nico and having some big nervous breakdown over how no one will ever love her. In which case, she's fine too.

Only why didn't she get someone to cover for her?

But my grandmother's tired and this is not the time for me to blather on about a girl I haven't hung out with in over a year. "I think she's okay," I say. "I haven't seen a lot of her lately."

"Hey there!"

"Hi."

Wendy stopped, not sure if she should or not. It had been three weeks since Jenny's party. We hadn't spoken since then. She had called once. I had not called back.

Now I said, "Nice sweater."

"Well, thank you." Someone said Hey, she nodded back, then asked me, "So, like—how are you?"

"I am good."

"Yeah, I see." She nodded. Then: "I'm sorry I . . ."

I shook my head. "Nah."

"Oh. Okay." She smiled uncertainly. "But we should—"

I cut her off. "Definitely."

There was a silence; then Wendy said brightly, "Saw you eating lunch with Rima the other day. Hanging with the top girls, whoa."

She smiled, because in spite of everything, she saw how funny that was, and for a moment, I almost smiled back. But I didn't.

Wendy sighed. "Well, bye . . ."

That was when I could have said, You know what, Wendy? You think you're hurting those girls who have so much power—and you are—but the one you're really hurting is you. And I wish you wouldn't because I like you so much. At least I used to.

I didn't say any of that. Instead, I thought, Why bother? She won't listen.

So I waved. *Bye.*

In the car, my mom says, "She needs to see people."

"Why? If she doesn't want to?"

"It's not healthy. You need to connect, interact, otherwise . . ." She turns the wheel. "By the way, when did your grandmother meet Wendy?"

"That winter," I say. "You were in Greece? Grandma came to stay? Wendy slept over."

My mom nods, remembering.

"Do you think she'll actually do it?"

Weirdly, last night was the first time I'd spoken to Wendy in forever. Even though we went to a lot of the same parties, we went for different reasons. I was the girl who listened. I was the girl who held people's heads when they puked. I was the girl who understood that you could love someone who treated you badly, that yes, it sucked when someone said they were skipping lunch and then you saw them eating with someone else, and that it was possible at sixteen to think you would never be happy. I never told anyone it didn't matter or asked why they cared. In fact, I never told anyone much of anything. I just watched and listened to the crazy.

And there was a lot of it, particularly when Wendy was at the party. And that night, people were hoping for more. I'd talked to Sean Pertwee about his mom's new boyfriend, who was only three years older than him. I'd listened to Deirdre Fish angst about her crush on her best friend, Melanie, who didn't seem to have a clue. And I'd nodded while Wilbur Pierce said his new meds were screwing up his head in a totally unfun way.

Every single one of them asked me the same question: *Do you think Wendy'll actually do it?*

And every single time, I said, I have no idea.

"I so don't get what guys see in her," said Layla Maxwell.

I do, I thought. I completely got it. Wendy would come at you with that total, out-there emotion and suddenly, you were a part of the coolest, most fun club in the universe. Wendy always seemed to know where life was, and if you were lucky, she'd grab you by the hand and take you along for the ride.

Funny, I thought. I'd forgotten that.

Around eleven, I was overdosed on people, so I ducked into the kitchen for a break. The kitchen was right by the front door; you could see people coming and going, or watch them through the window space that looked onto the living room. I was wearing what I always wore to parties: my favorite pair of jeans, tall boots, black turtleneck, and my signature army jacket with the I LIKE IKE button. Red hair up, two of Chinatown's best chopsticks stuck in the bun.

I found Wendy sitting on the windowsill. She had a plastic cup in her hand, one foot up on the sill, the other dangling toward the floor. And she was alone, which was strange. Wendy was never alone if she could help it.

In some ways, Layla was right. For a girl who got a lot of guys, Wendy wasn't that pretty. But she'd learned from all those top girls. She shopped where those girls shopped. She got her hair cut where they did. From a distance, she looked like a lot of thin, dark-haired girls in the city.

Up close was a different story. Up close, you saw her great smile. Up close, you felt her energy. Wendy was fun. Her friends loved it when she squirted ketchup packets in her hair as a joke. *Look, dye job!* Or pretended to have a fainting spell in H&M so someone else could snatch a few bracelets. A lot of people still didn't like her, but they paid attention to her.

But Wendy wasn't feeling fun that night. Maybe it was the way that dangling foot twisted like it was trying to find the floor. Or the way her fist sat pressed to her stomach. Or the way she breathed short little breaths like she was trying to get a grip on herself. She didn't want to be alone. Only, the one person she wanted to be with wasn't here.

Was she really going to do it?

The plastic cup was mostly ice by now, and she drained it. I said, "Hey, weren't you, like . . ."

Right away, she got the game. Do I Know You? We used to play it on people in the street. "Wait, wait, don't tell me."

"I saw you in that . . ."

"I heard your . . ."

"You were so great."

"You were, like, amazing."

We laughed. "Hey there." She got off the sill, gave me a hug. Wendy gave good hugs, long and strong.

"Hey," I said back.

"Seriously," she said. "How *are* you?"

"I'm cool, I'm good. . . ." I hesitated. "How are you?"

"I don't know, let me check with my multiple personalities. 'Good?' 'Yeah, all good, chief.' 'Good?' 'Just swell. . . .'"

She waved her hands. "No, good, I'm good."

I asked, "What's wrong?"

"Hm?" She looked confused.

"Wendy."

Wendy wandered over to the counter where people were dumping whatever bottles they had managed to steal from their parents or get someone to buy for them.

Pouring vodka into her cup, she said abruptly, "Have you ever been in love with completely the wrong person? I don't mean like he's shorter than you or doesn't have money or doesn't call . . ."

"Normal guy wrong."

"Right. I mean, like people could get hurt wrong." She started to pick up the cup, then put it down again. "What would you say to someone who was in love with someone like that?"

Love. This was new. Of course, I knew who we were talking about: Nico Phelps. Wendy's obsession with Nico was all over school. This year, her Facebook page was practically devoted to him. His body, his eyes, his clothes. Supposedly they'd gotten together a few times over the summer. But it didn't last. Nico dated up.

Wendy had sworn to make another play for him tonight. The fact that he had a girlfriend—and that girlfriend was Sasha Meloni—probably just added to the kick.

Most kids thought: *Wendy strikes again.* To me, the whole thing felt a little . . . frantic. Now I saw why. She was seriously hooked on this guy.

A memory of Nico flashed in my head. My stomach churned.

"I'd say, Stay away. Don't do it."

"What if you tried? What if it didn't work?"

"Try again? Wendy—"

I wanted to say, Please, stop this game. Stop before you get hurt. Or hurt someone else. Again.

The words were in my head. But they never reached the air. Before I could say them out loud, there was a group scream and the entire party seemed to surge toward the front door. The beautiful couple had arrived: Nico Phelps and Sasha Meloni.

Everyone wondered how Sasha would handle tonight. Would she even come to the party? Would she let Nico come? Anyone who thought she would bail didn't know Sasha. Sasha's mother is a ballet dancer. Her father something with money. Swanlike Sasha with her long body, cascade of auburn hair, and passion for art. She's not pool cleaner—and she's no doormat, either. A lot of people were hoping that Wendy was finally going to get what was coming to her. She'd messed with the wrong girlfriend this time.

In some ways, Sasha and Nico were an odd couple: Sasha so classy, Nico so bad boy. But I'd noticed that strange couples often paired up senior year. It was a last chance to try something new, experiment with a future self.

All eyes were on Sasha, Nico, and Wendy. As Sasha accepted fiercely loyal hugs from her friends in the hallway, I thought I saw her glance at Wendy through the entrance to the kitchen.

Wendy was watching Nico. Her energy was crackling, out of control.

Get her out of here, I told myself. Right now.

Wendy frowned, as if she had just remembered something. To me, she said, "Could you 'scoose me? Something I gotta do."

But she didn't leave right away. Instead she looked at me, mouth slightly open. About to tell me something—or hoping I would say something.

I opened my mouth. *Wendy, let's just get coffee. Eat some raw cookie dough.*

I never said it. And a second later, Wendy left the kitchen to find Nico. A little while later I left the party. 'Cause at this party, I'd seen the Wendy I'd really liked, the girl I thought would be my best friend till we were ancient.

But then she went racing after Nico Phelps and I didn't want to see what happened next.

"Thank God," my mom says, turning onto our street. "Home."

Home. Our building is called the Britannia, and it feels very

English; my mother says it's like living at Oxford. As I go into the building, I wave to the two gargoyles above the door, who I think of as Lola and Hubie. The first time Wendy saw them, she said they creeped her out.

It's after seven. As we unlock the apartment door and start turning on lights, my mom says, "We're ordering. You pick." She crosses to the answering machine, says, "Ugh." It's flashing furiously. I can guess: two of them will be Taylor.

Both with pretty much the same message. *Oh my God, did you hear what Wendy did?*

Also, I hope, one from Ms. Geller. *Good news, everything's all right.*

I've had to pee for the last half hour, so I go to the bathroom. Then I go to my room and take my cell phone out of my bag. Time to call Taylor and hear the whole horror story.

Taylor's number is ringing when there's a knock at the door. With a weird sense of déjà vu, I say, "Yeah?"

My mom opens the door. "Honey, I need to talk to you."

I'm listening for Taylor, show my mom the phone. In my ear, Taylor says, "Hey! Oh my God . . ."

My mom comes in, takes the phone from me. "Taylor? Hi, sweetheart. Can Rain call you back? Thank you, lovey."

"Mom!" I say as she hangs up.

She doesn't answer. Just sits on the bed, puts her hands on my shoulders. "This is going to be hard. And I want you to know I'm right here and I always will be. Are you listening? Did you hear that?"

"Yes, you're three inches away from me."

"Honey. Rain. They found her. In the park."

Why is my mom telling me this? I wonder. Who is *her*?

Oh, Wendy. Right. God, you spend a whole day thinking about someone . . .

Found her. They found her in the park. Playground. Swings. Kids. Good. So they found her in a nice place, not a motel, which was kind of what I was expecting.

Except . . . they? Not her mom?

They found her. I shake my head, because there's something weird about *found*. You find sweaters in the park. Or lost dogs. *Found* is like Wendy's not a person. Not a living . . .

My mom is crying. That tells me what *found* means. Why Wendy isn't a person anymore. That Wendy is dead.

Don't watch, my mom says. You don't need to see this.

But I do. I really do. I sit in front of the TV, watching people with microphones talk about Wendy. Or, not Wendy. The girl in Central Park.

On the TV, a reporter is standing outside the park walls. "There have been several attacks in the park in recent months. Cutbacks in housing and mental health services mean more mentally disturbed and drug-addicted people out on the streets. While police will not speculate, one wonders if this is just the latest tragedy in a larger trend of violent crime. . . ."

Why didn't I say something? I should have said something, I think numbly. Asked her to go somewhere. She wanted me to. That's why she hesitated.

"God," says my mom. "I hope her mother's not seeing this. They make you a thing."

I look up. "Should I call her?"

"Not now, baby." My mom sits down, hugs me for about the millionth time.

"I want to do something for her," I say. "I feel like I totally . . ."

I shake my head. My mom says, "What, honey? What?"

"I should have talked to her."

My mom looks puzzled.

"Wendy. I should have talked to her. I should have told her . . ." I take a deep breath. "I should have gotten her out of there. Only I *didn't*. And now . . ."

I throw my hand at the TV. My mom snaps it off with the remote.

Lifting my face, she says, "There was nothing you could do. I don't know how to say that so you'll believe it, but there was nothing you could do."

"I could have said—"

"What? Don't drink? Don't go to Central Park? Don't run into some creep who will hurt you? Honey . . ."

"Do you think that's what it was? Some crazy guy?" It's ridiculous but I can't stand the thought of Wendy being attacked by a stranger. I think of evil, hurting hands reaching out of nowhere. Wendy grabbed, the terror she must have felt.

"I don't know, honey, I have no idea. I don't think the park in the middle of the night is a good place for a young girl who's not thinking clearly."

She takes my hands in hers. "I do know: Wendy wasn't listening to anybody last night except Wendy."

But I was listening to Wendy, I think. I knew she wasn't okay. And I just left her.

The school sends out an email.

We will be marking the tragic loss of Wendy Geller with a special assembly tomorrow afternoon. Regular classes will be held as scheduled.

But we understand that students may wish to mourn in private. No student who wishes to stay home will be considered absent.

I can't sleep. Lying in the dark, staring up at the blankness of the ceiling, all I can think of is what it means not to be. The ceiling becomes a coffin lid, the sound of traffic outside a world I'll never rejoin. Am I breathing? Can I move? Panicked, I turn over, clutch at the blanket.

Once, when I was very little, my mom taught me a bedtime prayer. "If I should die before I wake . . ." I didn't want to say it. I imagined the universe saying, *Ah, she said it! Time's up! It's okay to take her.*

Take her. An unknown hand grabs you, and your life is over. How does that happen?

Rolling over, I try to feel what it means that Wendy is gone. That she's not at home, on the phone or watching TV. She's not at her dad's, or on the street, or . . . anywhere. I try to fix an image of Wendy in my head. Try to hear her voice. But already I can't. It feels like a second betrayal.

I get out of bed and turn on the computer. Three days ago, if you Googled Wendy Geller, you would have gotten maybe a few hundred hits, mostly Facebook stuff and Twitter. Now it's almost 100,000. WENDY GELLER Wendy Geller Geller, Wendy Wendy Geller Wendy Geller all over the screen.

I try to focus, click on News About Wendy Geller. My mom would want me to read the *Times* article, so I click on that.

A seventeen-year-old woman was found slain yesterday morning in Central Park. The police said she had apparently been sexually abused and strangled.

The body of the victim, Wendy Catherine Geller, was found by a jogger at about 9:30 A.M., according to Capt. Michael Fiske of the Manhattan 19th Precinct detective unit. Partially hidden, the body was discovered in a cluster of bushes in the Billy Johnson Playground, located at 67th Street and Fifth Avenue. "It was a cold, drizzly morning," said Lena Mosher, who regularly runs past the area. "I was out, but the playground was empty, thank God."

Ms. Geller was five feet, five inches tall with long brown hair. She was lying facedown in a garden circle in the center of the playground. She was wearing blue jeans and a red sweater. A black wool coat was on the ground nearby. Her clothes were disheveled. No weapons were found.

Ms. Geller attended Alcott School, a private school on Manhattan's Upper West Side. Family members say she was outgoing and well liked. "She had many friends," said her aunt Sonia Woolf, standing outside the building on East 73rd Street where Ms. Geller lived with her mother. "She loved fashion and design. This was a happy girl."

There have been several attacks in the park in recent months. Police are investigating the possibility that Ms. Geller's death might be part of a recent uptick in violent crime.

"You have a lot of mentally ill people in this city," said the victim's uncle, Louis Geller. "Nobody's watching them. People hurting for money, people on drugs. This is not a safe world." Ms. Geller's father, an attorney, lives in Garden City, Long Island, with her stepmother, Heidi Geller.

Ms. Geller was last seen at a party at a friend's house on East 70th Street. The police say they are still trying to determine what happened next.

There will be a gathering in Ms. Geller's memory later this week. Elizabeth Geller, the victim's mother, said, "A proper memorial will have to wait until the person who did this is caught. Then I'll know my daughter is at peace and we who loved her can celebrate her life."

I sit back, wondering. The police want to know what happened after the party. Does that mean they think someone at the party killed Wendy?

No, Rain, it means Wendy was killed after she was seen at the party. That's why they want to know what happened afterward.

I click on some of the other stories. The details are all the same. I find pictures, Alcott, Wendy's house, Central Park. A recent picture of Wendy smiling. Captured, blown up. Screaming words crowded around her image.

Wendy Geller Wendy Geller Geller, Wendy Wendy Geller Wendy Geller. The image starts to blur, the name becomes a meaningless sound. The more I look, the more Wendy fades. I try to get a fix on her laugh, the way her eyes narrowed as she smiled when she was about to make a not-nice joke, the way she suddenly giggled at herself when she'd done something dumb.

I'm losing her.

Quickly, I go to her Facebook page. I see she has a new photo since the last time I visited. Her picture used to be a close-up of her and her cat, curled up on her bed. Now it's some shot taken in a crowded restaurant. She's dressed in a short, spangled thing, wearing tons of makeup and laughing her head off.

I think, Personally, I liked the cat picture, Wen.

Already, the front page is filled with sympathy messages. All the stale, overused phrases people use when they don't know what to say: *My condolences to the family. So sad! Always in our hearts.* I think of writing something.

I miss you, Wendy. I'll always miss you. You were so . . .

I can't think of the right word. So . . . what? Sweet? Great? Amazing? I imagine people reading it and thinking, God, she couldn't come up with anything better than that?

Then I notice Videos. There are seven, which means I can actually see Wendy, hear her talk again. I click on the link, hit the first one in the row.

Wendy's face fills the screen. Then she pulls the phone back from her face and I can see she's in her bedroom. I hear something muffled from offscreen. Wendy turns and says, "I am, I swear to God!" The person off camera—a girl—laughs.

Then Wendy looks straight at the camera, composes herself. "Okay, here we go. Ready? Ready? Okay."

Clearing her throat, she says, "This is a message from Wendy Geller to Nico Phelps. Nico, you best be listening. Because two days from now at Karina Burroughs's party, I am going to get you. I am going to get you and you are going to love every moment."

She draws out the word *m-o-o-ment,* then does a big kiss to the camera. The person off camera shrieks, "Oh my God!" and starts clapping. Giggling, Wendy says, "Stay tuned for further details!"

Then black.

Further details, I think numbly. There are a lot of further details I would like to know, Wendy.

DAY TWO

It's Monday. The blast of coffee commercial on the radio tells me Get up, get out of bed, drag a comb across my head. I smack at it and it goes quiet.

I pull the covers over my head, hide in the warm dark.

Ten minutes later, the radio blares back to life. Sound pummels me through the quilt. "Police identified the body of a young girl found in Central Park . . ."

I burrow deeper.

". . . strangled . . ."

". . . assaulted . . ."

". . . one witness claims . . ."

". . . this latest attack . . ."

I throw off the covers, grab the radio with both hands. And howl. Long and hard and fierce. My ears hum, my throat starts to sting. But I can't hear the babble. I'm drowning it, killing it.

Then my mom's arms around me. The radio pulled from my hands.

"Shhh," she says, rocking me. "No more."

* * *

Last night on the phone, Taylor and I tried for about five minutes to actually talk about it. But then she said, "This needs to be face to face."

Now we're face to face in the Athens Diner on Broadway, where we always go because it's a few blocks from school, and we still don't know what to say.

Which is not like Taylor at all. Taylor is tiny: four feet eight, including her explosion of curls. She weighs maybe a hundred pounds. But that's just the physical. In terms of energy, Taylor is ten tons of sheer volume—as any school administrator who's ever tried to stop her from getting the real story knows. Cafeteria muffins not certified organic? Unequal funding for girls' and boys' basketball? School's stock investments support criminal regimes? Taylor's on it.

I order my second muffin—stress does not kill my appetite. Taylor asks for a refill on coffee.

Fingers over her mouth, Taylor says, "I wish I'd liked her more."

"She didn't die 'cause you didn't like her, Tay."

"No, I know." She picks up her coffee. "My mom's like, 'See, I told you, I told you there were crazy people out there. You think you're so tough, but it can happen to you.' I said, 'Mom, I'm not an idiot who goes into the park drunk in the middle of the night.'"

I look at her. Because Wendy didn't die because she was an idiot either. Wendy died because . . .

Those hands again, the ones I imagined last night. But no face. No reason. Just craziness tearing at you. Which makes me crazy. Not knowing why feels like staring into a bottomless pit; you feel dizzy, disoriented. Nothing makes sense and you could fall any second.

Taylor sighs. "I can't get close to the reality of it. That we'll go to school and she won't be there and the reason she won't be there is . . ." She frowns. "See?"

"The reason Wendy won't be there," I say, because Taylor didn't use her name, "is that she's dead. Wendy's dead."

The words still sound empty to me. They don't make any sense. I think of how long Wendy's been dead. What she's already missed. She missed that incredibly beautiful day yesterday. She didn't see a minute of it. Because she died before it got light. She died . . .

I feel Taylor's hand tight over mine. "Hey, baby."

I swallow. Shake my head.

"I can wait," says Taylor. "Actually, I'd be seriously grateful if you made me miss first period, because it's trig and guess who didn't do the homework?"

My throat eases up. I say, "I'm okay."

"Why should you be okay?"

To distract myself, I examine Taylor's bag. It's black, battered leather. On the strap, a small round pin. Black and gold, with a single letter: *E*. Alcott gives out four E pins every year to those who have excelled, exceeded, whatever *E* word you want to use. The school usually gets it right: people who get them have become judges and senators, won Oscars, Pulitzer Prizes. The real trick is wearing it without looking like a snob. Some kids even make a point of not showing them in public, they think it's obnoxious.

Taylor got hers last year, and I think she handles it just right. It runs in the family; her brother got one too. I've never gotten one—too shy. Wendy used to joke that the things she excelled at, they didn't give out E pins for.

"Tay?"

"Um, hm?"

"What happened? At the party Saturday. How did Wendy end up in the middle of Central Park at night?" Maybe, I think, if I know the whole story of Wendy's last night, what happened to her will make some kind of sense.

Taylor rolls her eyes: *Where to start?* "She was drunk, of course. I mean, sorry to speak ill of the hm, hm, but she was."

"She didn't seem *that* bad when I saw her," I say. "I mean, not so trashed that she'd go stumbling into the park in the middle of the night."

"She had on her little happy high." Taylor puts on a manic smile, bugs out her eyes. "The look that announces to anyone with half a brain that mayhem is about to ensue. And . . ." She stops.

"And what?"

Taylor shrugs, uncomfortable. "And also Nico was there and what else do you need to know? Wendy took one look at him and what working brain she had went *pop.*"

Now it's my turn to sit back. When Ms. Geller asked me if I had Nico Phelps's number, I almost said, Yes, it's right here, next to Satan's.

Most kids, I remind myself, like Nico. They invite him to their parties. They let him stay at their summer homes. Even Daisy Loring, who once accused him of stealing her mother's earrings.

Probably Nico's friends have a million stories about nice things he's done. Only those aren't the stories I've heard. And it's not the Nico I know.

Nico's not rich and he doesn't have famous parents. His mom's a home nurse and his dad, well, Nico usually calls his dad a loser and leaves it at that. He used to live in Queens before moving to Manhattan. But Nico does have two things. He's beautiful. I mean, ridiculous, with blond hair and blue eyes and a cleft in his chin. He's well built; a man's body, not a boy's. Supposedly, Nico's been approached by modeling agencies, he's that handsome.

And danger. Nico has danger. It's as if because he doesn't come from our world, he doesn't have to follow our rules. He breaks them, laughs about it, and everybody else laughs right along with him. So when he threw a drink in Kirsty Pennington's face, it was Ah, they were both kind of drunk. And when he got busted for drugs in the Hamptons—could have happened to anyone.

"So, what are you saying?" I ask Taylor. "Nico was mean to her or . . . ?"

Taylor shakes her head sharply.

"Well, what happened between them?"

Taylor shrugs. "Nothing, as far as I know."

This rings false. One thing you could be sure of with Wendy, when she promised drama, that promise was kept. I press. "Did you see them together at all?"

"Once. She was standing next to him, and they were talking."

"What was he like?"

"Did just enough to keep Wendy interested. You don't have to do much with her, let's face it."

I ignore Taylor's dig at Wendy. "Where was Sasha?"

Taylor drinks her coffee as she tries to remember. "Not with Nico."

Frustrated, I say, "You would have noticed if Wendy and Nico ended up making out on the couch, right?"

"There was no big drama explosion," Taylor says firmly. "Wendy split not that long after you—and from what I saw, she left alone."

"So, she didn't get Nico."

Taylor stares. "Did you ever think she would?"

I sit back. The image of Wendy on the screen—*I am going to get you and you are going to love every moment*—so much bravado. Her scampering over to Nico the second he arrived. I imagine his sneer as he turns away from her. Wendy backing off, shot down again. Top girls win, Wendy loses. One last diss, one last flush, one last cackle.

I need one person there that I know is on my side.

God, why didn't I stay?

I mash my mouth shut, trying not cry. Just then a woman comes up to us and says, "Excuse me?" We look up. "I'm so sorry, but I couldn't help hearing . . ."

When I was younger, I did speech therapy because the cleft palate screwed up my pronunciation. Endless hours of listening and repeating words and sounds. Maybe it's that, or maybe all the times I've listened to people "confess," but a lot of times when people talk, I don't hear the words. Because the words don't matter. What they're really saying is in the tone of their voice, or their eyes, or the way they hold their mouth. And when this woman says she couldn't help overhearing, I know she's lying. Her tense smile, the excitement in her voice—everything about her feels hungry.

"Did you know that poor girl? The one they found in the park?"

Taylor and I look at each other. I pick her to speak. Taylor says, "She went to our school."

"How terrible. Was she a friend?"

"Why?" Which is Taylor saying, Drop the act.

The smile slips. The woman nods: *Got me.* "I'm with the *Herald*, I don't know if you know—"

"I know it's garbage," says Taylor.

The woman doesn't even bother getting insulted. "I want to know who your friend was. We're hearing stories. Ugly stories. *Unfair* stories."

I ask, "What kind of—" Taylor does a quick head shake at me and I shut up.

Too late. The woman turns on me. "I want to get the truth out there before they trash her. That's all."

Trash her? Trash Wendy? Why? I'm frozen. I don't want to tell this woman anything and I want her to tell me everything.

I feel Taylor's hand on my arm, but I resist, wanting one little name, one fact.

"My card," says the woman, tucking it into my book bag. "Call me. I can help you help your friend."

Taylor pulls me out. As we spill onto the street, I hear the woman call after us, "Wendy can't speak for herself anymore. Speak for her! Speak for Wendy."

A block later Taylor lets go of my arm. Says, "Don't even think about it."

"No."

"In fact, give me the card."

I put my hand over my bag.

"Rain . . ."

"I'm okay."

"Great, give me the card."

But I'm not going to. As scummy as that woman was, the last thing she said to me was "Speak for Wendy." As if I have the power to do that. As if there's still something I can say that would help her. And I won't give up on that.

"I won't tell her anything," I say.

"You'll tell her things without knowing it," says Taylor.

"How? I'm not even going to call her."

"So."

But before Taylor can demand the card again, we turn the corner and see . . . an army. I mean, that's what it looks like. The Alcott School is a five-story limestone mansion—Taylor says it used to be a home for the rich and insane—nestled on a quiet stretch of Riverside Drive. Now it's under siege. Trucks and satellite dishes and cable, and a hundred people in the street. Cameras everywhere you look. Reporters with microphones. And kids, talking to the reporters.

"Oh my God," says Taylor. "How are we supposed to get through this?"

Wendy, I think as I walk through the halls. Where is Wendy?

Like Taylor said, it's so hard to get—really get—that Wendy isn't here. That she isn't anywhere anymore. Almost every spot, lockers, bathrooms, water fountain, is a space where Wendy used to be. Wendy groaning as she hoisted her backpack into her locker. Wendy dribbling water down her sweater, laughing, "I am *such* a total spaz." Wendy crying, "Oh my God, how ARE you?" before a huge swaying hug. Now I look at all those places and I see emptiness.

I want to talk about her, I think wildly. Right now. If she's not here, then I need to make her be here with words. I turn to a girl standing nearby—Fiona Robinson—and say, "God, remember how Wendy . . ."

Startled, Fiona steps back, says, "Sorry, what?"

She couldn't understand you. That's what crashes into my mind. *She heard, Ga, 'member how Wenny? and the poor girl's totally confused.*

I know I *didn't* say that. The speech therapy worked. I don't sound like that anymore. But the pause is long enough to make me feel stupid. Fiona wasn't really one of Wendy's friends. She might not know that Wendy and I were friends. She probably thinks I'm a creepy crisis junkie.

"No, nothing," I say, and do a little hi-bye wave as I hurry on.

Taylor has to get to the newspaper. I drift through the halls. No one's going to homeroom—and so far no one's making them. People are gathered in groups. Many are crying. I pass by a girl who's collapsing on her friend's arm as they hurry down the hall. Teachers are wandering, talking to people.

It's like after an earthquake, I think. People in a destroyed world; they don't have to run and hide, the immediate danger's past. But no one knows what to do now.

I walk past Wendy's locker, where people are gathering. There's a big ugly scar of police tape over it. On the floor, people have put bunches of flowers, stuffed animals. Someone's left a Starbucks cup, because Wendy was a caffeine addict. I smile at that.

I hear sniffling and turn to see a girl red-eyed and freaked. She can't take her eyes off Wendy's locker. She looks really young, I think she's a freshman. She couldn't have known Wendy. But she knows a girl just died and she doesn't know why.

I should say something to her, a Hey, it's okay.

But I can't. Because really, it's not.

I am not alone in trying to find out what happened that

night. There's a weird buzz, a hum, an Oh my God, and Did you hear? A lot of kids have their phones and iPads out. I spot Oliver Welks, who works on the paper, as he peers at his cell, then slow down to hear him say, "Another woman is saying she was attacked by a sicko in the park . . ." People immediately crowd him, wanting details.

I pass a group of guys by the water fountain. One says, "I'd never go to the park at night. My cousin did once. These guys jumped him, took all his stuff."

"Chick was seriously wasted," another says.

"Yeah, that probably didn't help."

On the stairs, a girl clatters past me, saying, "My sister's sick at home. She just texted me that when they found her, she didn't have clothes on." Her voice is almost gleeful.

There is outrage. Daisy Loring announces to her crew, "I just hope when they get the guy, they hurt him. I mean, because, you can't . . . you can't . . ." In my head, I finish her thought. You can't make someone like me feel scared and unsafe. Because I have never felt that way before and I don't like it. At all.

Then there are the kids who are out of it. The ones who either didn't know Wendy or have no group to swap rumors with or make pronouncements to. For them, it's just another party they weren't invited to. Some of them march past the groups, glaring angrily as if to say, Who cares? Some of them just wander, hoping they'll bump into someone. It occurs to me—that's basically what I'm doing.

And I do bump into someone. Wilbur, another lost soul, ambles over to me, head down like he's embarrassed. "Hey, dude," he says.

"Hey, Wilbur." I give him a hug. Wilbur's easy, one of the few people who's shyer than I am. He's not someone I can shove my feelings onto, but I can at least listen to him.

"It's weird," he says, looking around. "Like—I didn't know her, but . . ." He swallows hard. "She seemed sweet. Slightly twisted, but you know."

I smile. "Yeah, I do know. Stay mellow, okay?"

". . . trying," says Wilbur.

Then I run into Deirdre, sweet, chubby Deirdre, who says, "I can't believe it," over and over as if someone will tell her she doesn't have to.

She gulps, "I knew she lived on the edge, but this is way extreme." She looks around, lowers her voice. "Do you think it had anything to do with all that Nico stuff?"

I go still. "What do you mean?"

Deirdre squirms. "No, just she was a girl who pissed people off, you know? The way she went after everybody's guy? And she was way trashed that night. It's kind of like . . ."

Like she got what was coming to her. That's where Deirdre's going. She doesn't mean to, she'll feel bad about it later.

Rubbing her arm, I say, "It's beyond strange," and walk away.

Turning the corner, I see a huge crowd around Karina Burroughs. Karina who gave the party, Karina who always gives the party. She has a huge apartment. Her parents travel a lot and they don't ask questions.

I despise Karina Burroughs. Hate, detest, loathe, and any other word you want to use. She tortured me when we were kids. Her particular kick was to let her jaw go slack and make grunting noises whenever she saw me. Gorilla? Stroke victim? I was never sure. She can't get away with that these days. Supposedly, we're all more mature. She even has to let me into her parties, now that I'm seen as an official sane person.

Still, I slow down to listen. Because when you give the party, you know what went on at that party.

I'm good at being invisible; the group doesn't notice me at all. I know these girls. They replaced me in Wendy's life. They were the girls she gossiped with in class, the girls who laughed at her crazy stories in the cafeteria. *"So, then I was like, oh my God, Mr. Security Guard, I must have fainted! Of course I had the bracelet down my pants. Good thing no strip search. Although he was cute . . ."*

I hear Karina say, "The thing that kills me? Is let's face it. You knew it was going to happen. I mean, how many times did we say, Wendy—too much. You gotta chill out."

I know: these girls never told Wendy to chill out. They never told her, Too much. They laughed, they said, Wendy, you're insane! Maybe I didn't say things I should have to Wendy; but neither did they.

"And"—Karina lowers her voice—"of course she leaves this giant freaking mess behind. The cops called my parents in Europe, and they're like, Party? What party? So *I'm* totally busted."

I am dying to step forward, dying to say, "Yes, Karina, you're so right. The worst thing about Wendy's death is no more parties. Wow. How deep."

Just then I hear sobbing. Not Look at me, I'm so sad tears, but full-out crazy crying. I follow the sound down the hall and find Jenny Zalgat. Jenny who became Wendy's best friend after Wendy and I were done. I used to envy Jenny. Jenny was fun, Jenny got it about guys, Jenny didn't take it all so seriously. In my more evil moments, I thought, Jenny's about as deep as a piece of toilet paper, only not as smart.

Right now she's a wreck. She's leaning against the wall, her head hanging down, her hair in her face. Snot dripping from her nose, face red with tears. The sound of her crying is like vomit; you can tell it hurts to let it out. But she can't stop. Oh my God, she keeps saying over and over. Oh my God, oh my God. A few girls are standing around her, patting, making moo noises.

Slightly nervous, I approach, say, "Hey, Jenny . . ."

She pushes through the little crowd like I'm the one she's been waiting for and grabs hold. Startled, I wrap my arms around her, and for a moment we stand there, a soggy, miserable pair.

Jenny coughs. "She's not gone, right? Like, this is some horrible, disgusting nightmare. I just can't . . ."

I hug her tighter. The other girls drift away.

Jenny says, "I can't believe someone would do that. . . ." She stares off down the hallway and I can tell she's focusing on the stairs, the exit sign, whatever, to keep from losing it again. "She was the sweetest thing ever. You know? Would not hurt anybody. This makes no sense," she finishes forlornly.

"I know," I say. "She had a huge heart."

"Totally." She smiles, grateful that I get it. "Wendy always said you were the smartest person she knew."

"Ah . . ." That's all I can say. I had no idea Wendy even talked about me.

" 'Way too smart to be friends with me' was what she said." Jenny smiles sadly. "She was always putting herself down. And she *was* smart." She sniffs. "I'm so mad at her that she didn't know that."

"Me too," I say. The idea of being mad at a girl who's dead strikes us both as funny and we laugh—sort of.

Jenny says, "I feel like it's my fault." I must look puzzled, because she adds, "I left her, you know? I was her ride home, and . . ."

She breaks off, unable to say it. But she wants to tell me something about that night. If I press, she'll shut down. I just have to wait.

Then she blurts out, "I *would* have left with her, if she'd asked. But I thought . . . I mean, she told me . . ."

"What?"

She looks around, nervous that people are listening. "I don't want to say it. Everybody thinks she's Superslut as it is."

"I don't think that, Jenny."

"No, I know." She lowers her voice to barely a whisper. "Just . . . I thought she was leaving with Nico."

A chill goes right down my spine, even as I think, No. Not possible. Taylor said Wendy left alone, and Taylor does not get her facts wrong.

Only she didn't say she knew it for a fact. She said *from what I saw.*

And while Taylor is way smarter than Jenny about most things, the one subject where Jenny's got the edge is Wendy.

"Why'd you think that?" I ask, keeping my voice low so Jenny feels safe.

Jenny sniffs as she remembers. "At the party, I saw Wendy talking to Nico. I saw Sasha . . . nowhere. Like she'd just given up. Next thing I know, Wendy comes up to me all hyperexcited and says, 'Leave, split, I'm cool.' I was like, Yay, call me tomorrow with the juicies."

"Did you actually *see* Nico and Wendy leave together?"

She thinks. "No. Zoe Wavel wanted to do a cab, like, that second, and I had to zoom."

"So what do you think happened?"

"I don't know," she wails. "I don't know and it's making me crazy. I mean, I guess he blew her off at the last minute. Which would completely freak her out. So she went . . ."

Into the park. Upset, drunk. Wearing shoes she couldn't run in. Expensive clothes. The perfect victim.

Now I lay me down to sleep.

A question is forming in my head, but before I can bring it into focus, Jenny says, "I think I'm going to get out of here. I thought it'd be better, being with people who knew her?"

But they don't, so it's not. I nod. "Yeah, sure."

She takes a few stumbling steps, then turns. "Guess I'll see you at the . . ."

It takes me a moment to understand. Funeral. Wendy's funeral. The thing they do before they burn you or put you in the ground to rot.

"Yeah," I manage to say to Jenny.

I have to go into the bathroom after that. For a long time, I just sit in one of the stalls, eyes closed, head buried in the V of my arms. Little bits of random fact float around my brain. The expression on Wendy's face when I saw her in the kitchen. *"Have you ever been in love with completely the wrong person?"* The jolt of energy when Nico walked in the door.

Is Nico in school today? I don't remember seeing him.

A possibility: Wendy says come be with me. Nico says no. She gets freaked, gets trashed, and wanders into the park.

But no, Wendy was happy. Jenny said so.

Come be with me, Nico.

Nico says yes . . .

One of the things about staying quiet? You think too much. All that chatter that normal people share gets bottled up in your head. And you start thinking the craziest things because, hey, it's not like you're going to say them out loud.

Nico says yes. They go into the park, and—

No. I cut myself off abruptly. I don't like Nico. I think Nico's a jerk. But there's a big difference between jerk and . . .

The outer door opens and I jump. I hear the soft sound of a bag being settled on the sink. Carefully unlocking the door, I go out, hoping I can sneak past before whoever notices me.

"Whoever" is Sasha Meloni.

She's shaking out her mane of hair, a clip in her teeth, and when she catches my eye, there's a spark of humor. *Yes, me, beautiful Sasha, I hold my hair crap in my mouth like everybody else.*

Or maybe it's *I'm such a dork, please don't tell.* Sasha Meloni could secretly think she's a dork—but I doubt it. For one thing, she'd be wrong. And Sasha is not usually wrong.

Normally, the sight of someone as prima as Sasha would send me scuttling out the door. But despite our vast differences in school status, Sasha and I have this odd little connection because of our moms. There aren't a lot of people who get the weirdness of having a mother who calls Lincoln Center the office. Sasha's mom doesn't dance anymore, but she fund-raises for New York City Ballet. Sasha and I have been at a few of the same events. There's a guard at Lincoln Center we both hate, a dancer we both think is to die for—even though, as Sasha said, "I don't think either of us has a chance." At the time, I thought

Wow, beautiful Sasha, nice Sasha, to pretend we would ever have the same chance with a guy.

So, does Sasha look like a girl who lost her boyfriend to the school skank Saturday night?

No, she does not.

But Sasha is not the kind of girl to look like that girl.

For a moment, we both fix our hair—Sasha brushing, me re-arranging ornamental chopsticks. Like Taylor, Sasha has an E pin. Only she had hers set in a ring, black and gold on her long, strong fingers. I'm sure she got the pin for art; she's a sculptor. A seriously good one. No hiding for Sasha; she puts her elite status right out there for everyone to see.

Then Sasha says, "Strange day, huh." Her voice is deep, not accented, but exotic somehow. Sophisticated. As if she speaks many languages, keeps many secrets. You have to work hard to read Sasha.

"It certainly is," I say. Then, taking a chance to see how she's feeling about Wendy: "Are you going to the assembly later?"

"I don't know. It's awful what happened . . ." Hair done, she's putting on lip gloss. "But it's all kind of fake, you know? The crying and . . ." She waves her hands in the air.

I wait for her to say the words: *Slut stole my boyfriend. Why should I care?*

But she doesn't.

She picks up her bag. "I'll probably go. It would be tacky not to." So Sasha—not rude, not cold, *tacky.*

Then she frowns. "It's just . . . all the stupid *drama.*" Angry, she pokes in her bag. "People with no lives, you know?"

Realizing what she said, she sighs. "Yeah, well."

Then: "I'm sorry; you knew her, right?"

"Right."

She nods slightly, makes a guilty little *click* with her tongue. "Well, I'm really sorry." She holds up a hand as she leaves. "Ciao."

"Ciao." The door swings shut.

I walk out of the bathroom to find the halls quiet. People have started heading to the assembly. Then I see Rima Nolan by her locker.

Rima and I were friendly for a little while after our chat on the stairs. But then I moved on to Taylor, and Rima moved on to Sasha. These days, we mostly do the hallway hi thing.

Over the summer, Rima traded her dark Brontë tresses for a short, chic bob. Now she's a flapper in Paris, a silent-film star, or one of those eerie children in a Japanese horror movie.

"Hey, Rima."

She smiles. I pause, wait for her to say something. *God, so sad. Really horrible.* But she doesn't.

I wait for myself to say something. *This must be kind of weird for you, Rima.* But I can't tell where Rima is, what she's feeling.

Still smiling, she says, "Ding dong. The bitch is dead."

She walks past me and down the stairs.

"Hey, hey." In the crowd, a hand reaches out, pulls. Taylor hugs me. "Found you."

As we climb the stairs, Taylor fumes, "Dorland won't let me write word one about the murder. A nice 'We Remember' article on the front page, and something about safety tips—that's it. The whole world's on this story and I can't touch it, because he doesn't want Alcott to look bad. Can you believe it?"

I can. Emile Dorland. The headmaster of Alcott. A man who

lives surrounded by books. My mother swears he taught at the school when she went there, and while I think she's kidding, he does seem to live in another world, alongside Shakespeare and Tennyson. He never calls students by their first name, it's always Ms. or Mr. His primary human contact is his ancient secretary, Ms. Laredo.

Then Taylor says, "The police are here. I saw them outside Dorland's office."

"Do you think they caught the guy?"

Taylor shakes her head. "No news when I last checked, and that was, like, five minutes ago."

"Right." Still, I can't help hoping the police will make an announcement. *"I'm happy to report that we have a suspect in custody. . . ."*

Or maybe it's not an announcement. Maybe the police are here because they suspect someone at the school.

Taylor says, "Poor Laredo was taking all these calls from parents. 'The school's doing everything we can to keep your child safe.'" Her voice goes high and quavery as she imitates Ms. Laredo. "Parents are going nuts. Like the killer's walking the halls or something."

As we come into the assembly hall, I see the stage and catch my breath. To one side of the podium, someone's placed a table. On it, a framed photograph of Wendy and a small votive candle.

"Where do you want to sit?" asks Taylor. "Back or—"

"Front," I say. I want to be near Wendy's picture.

The hall is packed. The entire upper school is here; well, at least everyone who came to school today. I keep an eye out for Nico, wanting to see: does he look sad? Smirking? Nervous?

Is he with Sasha? Are they really just fine? But I don't see him anywhere.

"No sign of Nico," I say, wanting Taylor's take.

"Yeah, like he'd miss a chance to ditch."

Taylor is probably right, I think. No huge guilt, just a day off school.

I hear Taylor say, "Oh, God."

"What?"

"Ellis."

She nods and I see Ellis Patel standing on the sidelines with his friends. He's sobbing so hard, his shoulders are shaking. His best friend, Lindsey Adams, has her arm around him, while Leo Berger and Bonnie McDermott pat his arm, stroke his hair.

Ellis Patel. Wendy's last—maybe only—real boyfriend. They started dating at the beginning of this year. Ellis is a senior, Wendy a junior, and it was another weird senior year couple. But a good one. I remember thinking, Finally, someone who doesn't belong to somebody else! Ellis is not only cute with the black hair, and captain of the chess team smart, he's also laid-back and has a totally goofy sense of humor. In that way, he and Wendy were the perfect match.

But a month ago, Wendy broke up with him.

I check out Daniel Ettinger, who hooked up with Wendy in ninth grade. He's smiling and laughing with Fredo Lowell, as if we're all here to hear about fire drills. Malcolm Liddell—he's sitting with his arm around his girlfriend, staring off into space. Cute Seth with the shoulders seems to have cut along with Nico. All these guys knew Wendy. Not one of them is crying for her today. Only Ellis—the one she dumped. I look back, wish there was something I could say to him.

At that point, Mr. Dorland steps up onto the stage. The man is struggling. He's probably in his sixties, and it looks like he turned eighty overnight. As he places his hands on the podium, I notice them shaking. His eyes, as he looks out at us, are blinking and nervous.

In a tentative voice, he says, "Before I begin, I would like to introduce Detective Sergeant David Vasquez." He nods to a small, bald man who raises his hand in greeting. "He is investigating this matter. Some of you have spoken with him and his team already. He may wish to contact others at a later date. I trust you will give him your full cooperation."

A murmur goes through the crowd as people try to figure out who has been contacted, who will be contacted, and what it all means. I make my own list: Karina, maybe Jenny. I feel a lurch of anxiety: will they want to talk to me?

"And so you left your friend at this party, when you knew she was in trouble?"

"Yes, yes, I did, Officer."

Then Mr. Dorland tells us we can visit Ms. Callanan, the school shrink, if we need to. She stands and waves a little too eagerly, as if she's excited to get her hands on all this emotion.

"Special teams of counselors will also be assisting Ms. Callanan in this task." Then, bowing his head, Mr. Dorland says, "Finally, we turn our attention to the true reason we are here today: remembering Wendy Geller."

I sit up, as if Wendy, wherever she is, can see me and know

that remembering her is important. It occurs to me: I don't know if I believe in heaven.

"Students, this is a terrible day at Alcott. A young woman's life has been taken, and we who knew her are left to grieve the loss. I . . . I confess I cannot quite believe it." He glances toward the closed doors of the assembly hall. "I expect to see Ms. Geller walking in at any moment."

I feel a ripple in the crowd, an energy wave of agreement. From some parts of the room, sniffing, a sob.

Then Mr. Dorland says, "Ms. Geller was relatively new to our school, and while I knew her, of course, and admired her wonderful spirit—"

Fake, I think without wanting to. Wonderful spirit—it's something a teacher says about someone they didn't know. Or didn't like.

Mr. Dorland starts talking about loss. He quotes a poem. But none of it feels like Wendy. Which I guess he realizes because he finally says, "I wonder if now is the time for those who knew Ms. Geller to come forth and say a few words."

Now the wave has a different energy. Anxiety. Awkwardness. Mr. Dorland's been so uptight and formal, no one wants to follow him.

Taylor nudges me, but I shake my head. I do not do public speaking. When I was ten, my mom dug up these old home videos and got them transferred to disc. I was all excited. Ooh, I get to see myself as a little kid.

Then I saw this three-year-old running around, yelling, "–i, Mom. 'Ook a me."

My mom was getting all misty, saying things like "You were so cute!" And all I could think was Why didn't I know I sounded retarded? Why didn't anybody tell me? How could she put me out in the world sounding like that?

But someone has to speak for Wendy. Jenny's gone home. Ellis looks too broken up to say anything. I think of all the girls who thought Wendy was so "hilarious," the boys who thought she was "hot." Why won't they speak for her?

Well, why won't you, Rain? Wendy was the one person who said your cleft palate didn't matter, so why are you letting that stop you? Raise your hand.

But I can't. My pronunciation is much better than when I was little. But when I imagine myself talking, all I can hear is *Wendy wash a 'ood fend.*

Raise your hand, Rain, I order myself. I chant this over and over in my head. But my hand doesn't move.

Mr. Dorland is looking around the room. The longer the silence goes on, the weirder it gets. Now even someone who might have wanted to say something feels strange.

Then I hear, "I'd like to say something, Mr. Dorland."

A man's voice, not a kid's. Light, precise, intelligent. I don't even have to look to know. It's Mr. Farrell.

"Go for it, tigress."

All of a sudden, Wendy's in my head, vivid, real, laughing. Only it's two years ago and we're standing in the hallway outside history when Mr. Farrell comes out of his classroom. He's rushing down the hall, but stops to nod to us. "Good afternoon, ladies."

And when he's gone, I say, "Now, *he's* hot."

I don't actually want the word *hot,* though. I want the word *beautiful.* I want *tall,* want *lean.* I want to say, I didn't know how to want until the universe showed me T. H. Farrell.

Wendy would laugh if I told her that. Which is why I say "hot."

But Wendy gives me a long, strange look. As if my choice reveals just how little I know about men and sex. As if I had said, "I want to date Luke Skywalker."

Embarrassed, I mumble, "I'm just saying . . . if I had to pick someone at school."

Wendy snaps out of her stare and smiles. "No, no, I get it. Not my type, but he's sort of . . ." She pauses as she looks again.

Then she does laugh. "Hey—why not? Go for it, tigress."

"Yeah, he's a teacher. Not to mention married."

"Oh, like that matters."

I miss you, Wendy, I think as Mr. Farrell replaces Mr. Dorland at the podium. Right now, if you were here, you'd be whispering, "Sit up, lady. Show yourself." And I'd tell you, Quit it, but I'd love that you were trying to make me try.

I look up at Mr. Farrell. Dark hair, huge gray eyes. A face that's somehow Irish and Native American both. He's a little nervous to be speaking in front of this big a crowd, you can tell. Maybe because he went to Alcott when he was a kid, sometimes he seems a little more one of us than a teacher. Kids like him, which is probably why Mr. Dorland made him acting head of the upper school when Ms. Johnson went on maternity leave. I've never had him for class. Taylor has him this year. I try not to be in total agony that he will fall madly in love with her.

He starts off by saying, "Wendy Geller was not my best student. In fact, I think the first thing I ever said to her was 'If you have something to share, Ms. Geller, please share it with all of us.'"

People laugh. Part of the problem has been Dorland talking about Wendy as if she were some nice white-bread girl, just because she's dead. It feels good to remember how ditzy she could be.

Now Mr. Farrell says, "Wendy was a person who had a lot to share." He pauses. "Even if she didn't always pick the best times."

Or the best people, I think.

"She had laughter, she had warmth, she had a . . . genuine caring. I often felt bad that she didn't seem to realize how rare those qualities are, how special."

I find myself nodding. Mr. Farrell sees me, smiles a little. I smile back.

Then Mr. Farrell drops his head as if what he's feeling is too private to show. "I don't want to talk about how we lost Wendy, about . . . anger and . . . rage and . . . stupidity. I would rather be grateful that Wendy did share her laughter and her love with so many of us. And feel sad that she will not be able to share them with the rest of the world."

I'm crying. Taylor's staring into the distance, trying not to cry. And we're not the only ones. Someone's finally said: *Hey, this girl wasn't perfect, but I liked her. I'm really mad that she's gone.* All around, I can feel the energy's opened up. No more embarrassment or fakeness. Just sorrow. Loss. The things that really are. I look at the photograph on the table, the little light flickering in front of it. The big brown eyes and the friendly smile. *Hi there!*

Wendy.

Later, as we file out of the hall, I notice there's a table with flyers on it. Wendy's picture in grainy black-and-white. If we know anything, we're supposed to contact the police.

Why? I wonder. If the killer was some random crazy guy, why ask us?

* * *

61

I'm standing outside Mr. Farrell's room. The school is mostly empty. Most people cleared out after the assembly.

I have never spoken to Mr. Farrell. My tongue is twisted up with nerves, and for a moment, I feel panicked that an ugly mess will come spitting out of my mouth. *Mithder Faruhl?* Not that he would be mean about it. If anything, he would be horribly kind.

So what? I hear Wendy say. *Take it from me, babes. You only live once.*

Impulsively, I knock on the door. A weird moment of silence. Maybe I was wrong. Maybe he's gone home.

Then I hear, "Come in."

Mr. Farrell's is one of the smaller classrooms, with high windows on one side. Most teachers cover the walls in pictures and posters, but his are plain, just the white plaster and dark wood molding. To look, you don't know; are you in a German class? Trig? Art history? Mr. Farrell teaches English, but there's nothing in the room to tell you that.

In the center is a big round table. Mr. Farrell is sitting near the window. There are papers on the table. But it doesn't look like he's touched any of them.

I stay half in the hallway as I say, "Mr. Farrell? I don't know if you know me, but . . ."

He smiles. "Rain, of course I know you." He gestures. "Come on in. You can shut the door."

How happy this makes me, that he lets me in, says close the door, as if we need privacy. You're sad, I tell myself, really sad. But it doesn't stop me from being happy.

Of course, now I have to speak.

"I, uh . . ." I had words. I rehearsed them on the way here. They were perfect, wise, mature . . . and now they've vanished. "I . . ."

He pulls out a chair. "This has been a very hard day. Why don't you sit?"

I do. It's both better and worse. Better because I'm near him. Worse because I'm near him. Wendy, I think. I'm here to talk about Wendy.

I mumble, "What you said about Wendy . . ."

"Yes." I like how he says just enough to fill in the blank spaces, but not so much that I feel rushed.

"I'm really glad you said it." Now I can look at him. "You know, that somebody did."

He coughs a little, pushes at the papers. "Well, I appreciate that, because I thought it was pretty . . . inadequate." He smiles, and that connection I always knew was there—two people scared to speak—hums between us. "I thought any friend of Wendy's would think, Who does this guy think he is?"

"I was friends with Wendy, and that's not what I thought."

"Oh," he says, clearly surprised. "I didn't know that."

"It was a long time ago." He filled my silence before; now it's my turn. "I know, people think, Hm, pretty different . . ."

"No."

"But that was one of the things that was sort of great about Wendy. She didn't . . ." I'm not putting it right. "She wanted to be popular? But she wouldn't put other people down. She was into status, but she wasn't a snob. Actually, she could get pretty fierce when people were snobby to her."

"I wish you had said that at the assembly."

Immediately, I shake my head. "Public speaking and me . . ."

"Why not?" he asks.

I check his face. He's serious; he has no idea why I would be afraid to speak. It makes me think of Wendy in my kitchen: *Give up the silence.*

For no reason, I blurt out, "I already can't remember what she looked like."

"That happens," says Mr. Farrell. "When my dad died, I kept all these pictures of him on my desk, so I could have him fixed in my head."

I have this horrible impulse to tell him that I don't have any pictures of my dad. That I might not even know when he dies.

Mr. Farrell's briefcase is open on the table. Inside the top, there's a photo of a little boy. Just past baby. He has big happy eyes and brown hair. He's crazy about whoever he's looking at, you can tell from his face. Total love.

"That's your little boy?" I ask.

"Nathaniel." He moves the briefcase so I can see better.

"So cute."

"Thank you." He glances at the picture. "He . . . Well, he's mine. So he must be the most wonderful, perfect kid ever born, right?"

"That's how dads should feel," I say.

Looking at the picture of Nathaniel and thinking of Wendy reminds me of Ms. Geller. She has the same picture of Wendy—hundreds of them, I'll bet.

Without thinking, I say, "I said totally the wrong thing."

"When?"

"Wendy's mom called me. That morning. She wanted to know if I knew where Wendy was. And I was all like, Oh, she's fine, don't worry. Now I feel horrible."

He leans in. "That's what she needed to hear, Rain. You sensed that, so you gave it to her. There's nothing wrong with that. It was kindness."

I shake my head. "*You* should call Ms. Geller. Tell her what you said."

He smiles, breaking up the sadness. "What, that her daughter talked too much in class?"

"*No.*" I smile back. "The part about Wendy laughing, caring. That stuff. She'd like that."

"Really?" He looks unsure, and I love that he's so cool and doesn't know it.

"Really," I say. "Hey, made me feel better."

He laughs. "Well, then I'm really glad I said it."

I twist my hands together. "Mr. Farrell?"

He leans in. "What?"

"I don't want to gossip or anything. But . . . do you know what the police are . . . ? Like, if they have a suspect? You probably can't tell me things like that."

"I can't," he says gently. "Because I don't know myself. They're keeping a very tight lid on this."

"Why were they here?"

He considers his answer; I wonder what he might be hiding. "Primarily so that Mr. Dorland could introduce Detective Vasquez. We felt it would be easier for students if they saw him before they got a call from the police."

"Do you know who they're calling?"

He shakes his head. "Why?"

I stare down at the ground. "No, I just hope they talk to people who . . ." I look up. "Not everybody liked Wendy. Some people are into trashing her, saying, like, she deserved it, 'cause she . . ." I wave my hand, not wanting to list the reasons people think Wendy deserved to get killed.

Mr. Farrell says, "When disaster strikes, people get scared. They want to find a reason it won't happen to them. Something the victim did wrong that they would never do."

"Yeah." I nod gratefully. "I think there's a lot of that going around." Then in a burst, I add, "It's like when people pick on a kid, they know it's wrong? But they always find some reason the kid deserves it. . . ."

Too much. Way too much. I stop talking, stare at the floor. What am I doing, blathering like this?

I mumble, "I guess I'm just freaked by the whole thing."

"Of course." A pause. "Do you feel like you could talk to Ms. Callanan?"

I shake my head. Freshman year, when I was having a really rough time, I went to her once. All she did was grip my hand and say things like You must feel so SAD. You must feel so ALONE. I was like, Well, yeah—and?

"I think I have to get through it myself," I say.

"No, you don't," he says.

Something in that statement gives me the guts to look up. We sit there looking at each other. It occurs to me that if the silence lasts one more second, he will know how much I like him and this will go from wonderful to deeply embarrassing.

Actually, he probably already knows and the only thing left is to show him that it's cool, I'm not a moron.

So I get up. "I've wasted a lot of your time."

"You have not," he says.

"Well . . . at any rate"—I start toward the door—"thank you again and . . ."

"Rain?"

"Yes."

He hesitates. "You're welcome. First. And . . ."

I wait.

"Come talk to me anytime."

"Okay." He doesn't mean it. I do get that. He's being nice.

"And I'm not just being nice."

I laugh. "Okay." Wanting this to last, I glance at the bare walls. "You don't like pictures?"

"I don't like pictures," he says, grinning. "I like words. When people are in my class, I want them to listen. Really hear the words and feel the emotion. Not get distracted by a picture of the person or their life. Listening—it's an old-fashioned concept, I know."

"Yeah, I do know."

He smiles.

Most Alcott kids live near school, in the Seventies and Eighties, either on the pretty wealthy West Side or the flat-out rich East Side. I live on 110th, up near Columbia University, which is a different scene. My mom got a huge apartment there when she wasn't making a lot of money. The neighborhood's changed since then, but a lot of professors and writers and artists still live here. My mom says she'll never leave because this is where she brought me home after I was born. Plus our building has gargoyles. "How can I leave the gargoyles?" she asks. Not to mention St. John the Divine, the Hungarian Pastry Shop, and V & T's, which has the best pizza in the city.

As I walk, I think about what Mr. Farrell said about Ms. Callanan. Maybe I should try again. The thing is, the one time I saw her, she was so busy feeling sorry for me, she never even heard why I was there in the first place. I feel like I could have told her exactly what happened with Nico in the stairwell and she still would have gushed on about SAD and LONELY. She would have made it about me and not him.

Right after the thing with Nico, I thought about it every day. I would play it over and over in my mind; what Nico said was always the same. What he did was the same. But in my imagination, I fought back.

Which was not what happened, of course.

I haven't thought about it in a while. Now the whole rotten memory comes back in a rush like vomit.

"Come on, I want to see."

It was in ninth grade, during that not-great time when my two friends, Layla and Sophie, had left. I would walk/run through the halls, praying no one would speak to me. It had been years since kids deliberately said hello just so they could make fun of whatever I said back. But why risk it?

So why did I risk it with Nico Phelps? Maybe because he was new to the school. A year older than me, he'd never made fun of me. Probably because he had no idea who I was—but still. I knew who he was, of course. Everyone knew Nico Phelps, the moody blond guy whose worn cashmere sweaters stretched tight across the elbows and shoulders.

I'd noticed those sweaters. They were expensive, but not new. Hand-me-downs? Not something you saw at Alcott every day.

I think that's why, when he said hello that afternoon on the stairwell, I felt . . . excited. Happy. I was on my way to chorus practice. We were alone on the stairs, one of the smaller, windowless stairwells that leads down to the basement. They're old-fashioned, cramped. I remember thinking, Yeah, he would want to wait till no one was around. He is breaking the rules by talking to me.

Which is why I said "Hi" back.

"Rain, right?"

He knows my name, I trilled to myself. He cares who I am.

"Right. And you're Nico."

He smiled, *Um-hm.* Then said, "I want to see the hole."

I didn't get it right away. His voice was still friendly, his shoulders relaxed. I felt no threat; it just didn't make sense.

I must have shaken my head, because he continued, "They say you've got a hole in your mouth. That's why you talk like a retard."

Even then, I accepted it. He wasn't being mean, just explaining. It was what people said about me. I had a hole in my mouth, I talked like a retard. It was the way it was. How could I be hurt by that?

Maybe, I thought, the hole is like his sweaters. The way they don't fit right.

"Come on," he coaxed. "I want to see."

And so I did it. I opened my mouth. I even tipped my head back to give him a better view. That's how much I wanted to believe this was about connection. Not humiliation.

Nico leaned down—he was taller than I was. For a moment, his curiosity felt real, as if he were looking at a scar left by a car wreck. His gaze made me feel ugly—but powerful. I thought of saying, "When I was born, I didn't have a roof to my mouth. There was just this little ridge of tissue. So they puullled a little from one side, puullled a little from the other, and kind of tied it all together. But there wasn't enough. And that's why the hole. There's a space where it doesn't connect."

When he stood up, the little smile was back. Lifting his hand, he pointed a finger, then stuck it in my mouth. He wiggled it roughly, the knuckle knocking against my teeth, the nail scratching. A taste—blood or the salt of his skin? A fingertip, blunt and rough, worked its way into the shallow indentation, pressed hard. Harder. A brief terrible moment of no air.

Panicked, I twisted away, batted uselessly at his arm. He pulled the finger out.

For a moment we just stood there. Jumbled, upset, I thought, Will he apologize? Kiss me? What?

He said, "Aw," in a long sneer that felt like a snake slithering heavily across my body. Then he continued down the stairs.

I thought of crying. But who would listen? In the end I just went home.

Turning on 110th Street, I imagine the park at night. Tree branches waving against a dark sky. Buildings towering over you, windows blank and indifferent. Streetlights to brighten the path—but not the shadow areas among the trees and bushes.

How long were you without air, Wendy? I wonder. Did you scream? Could you scream? In the darkness with those hands around your throat? Did you pray someone would hear? Pray they would come running and help you?

After a while, there probably was no air. And no sound.

Just the silence as he finished.

My phone buzzes. Taking it out, I see it's my mom. "Hey, Mom."

"Hi, honey. Listen, sweetie?"

"Yeah?"

"The police would like to talk to you."

* * *

"Just tell them what you know."

"I don't know anything."

My mom squeezes my hand. "Honey."

It's evening, but we haven't eaten dinner yet. Just as well. Food would never make it into the twisted mess that is my stomach right now.

A moment ago, the buzzer rang. It was the police. Any second, they'll ring the doorbell.

"They're taking a long time," I say. "Maybe they got lost."

The doorbell rings. Hurrying to answer it, my mom says, "They're just going to ask you some questions."

Just, I think. Questions mean answers. Which I don't have.

I hear my mother say, "Detective . . . ?" Murmurs back and forth as she lets him in. Then: "My daughter's in the living room."

They appear, my mother and the detective. It's the guy from the assembly, Detective Vasquez. He is rounded and bald. When he comes close, I see that his skin is pockmarked. I like him for that.

"My name's Detective Vasquez." He raises his hand awkwardly. "Good evening, Ms. Donovan." Which sounds very weird; Ms. Donovan is my mother, not me.

As he sits down, I say, "You can call me Rain. I mean, if you want."

"Rain," he says easily. "So, Rain. First of all, I'd like to thank you for speaking with me."

"You're welcome." My mother sits down next to me. The detective notices that.

He opens his hands. "Is there anything you would like to tell me to begin with? Anything you'd like to ask?"

"Just . . . I don't know. The obvious. Do you know who—?"

"No," he says promptly, "but we're doing everything possible to find the individual, I promise you."

He says that to everyone, I think. To Wendy's mom, her dad, the newspapers.

Shifting slightly in his chair, he gets down to business. "I understand you attended the same party as Ms. Geller that evening?"

I nod, wondering who told him. Wendy's mom, I bet. *A very reliable girl, Detective. You'll want to speak to her.*

"Did you speak with her at all?"

"Yeah, a little."

"Can you tell me what you talked about?"

Have you ever been in love with completely the wrong person? Part of me really wants to tell the detective about Wendy's insane crush on Nico. But I don't want to add to the crazy slut story. I want the police to know about Nico—but I don't want them knowing it from me.

"Don't worry about me," says my mom. "Just say whatever it was."

I smile weakly. Then say to Detective Vasquez, "No, it was girl stuff. Party talk. Boys."

"Any boy in particular?"

His voice is casual; I can't tell what he's heard about Nico. "Well, you've looked at Wendy's Facebook page, right?"

"We're aware of it."

"So, you know she liked Nico Phelps." I'm not sure; does he nod or not? But he's writing it down.

As he writes, I get up the courage to ask, "Have you talked to Jenny Zalgat?"

He flips through his notebook, nods.

"Jenny said she thought maybe Nico and Wendy left the party together. Did she tell you that?"

"We have several witnesses who say that Ms. Geller left the party alone that night."

"Oh." So, Jenny was wrong. Wendy didn't get Nico.

Abruptly switching tone, Detective Vasquez says, "Can I ask if you observed anything else about Ms. Geller that night?"

"Like what?"

"Well, for example, did she seem intoxicated to you? High?"

Startled, I say, "No."

"Can you tell us if she took drugs of any kind?"

"No, I can't. Why do you want to know?"

He shrugs. "A young woman ends up in the park late at night—we need to know her state of mind, that's all. Some of the other kids at the party indicated that Ms. Geller was maybe . . . a little altered."

"Not when I saw her," I say firmly. I'm not even sure that's the entire truth; but if people are blaming Wendy for what happened, I don't want any part of it.

"Okay," he says easily. "Anything else?"

I struggle. Something more needs to be said.

"Just . . . Wendy wasn't stupid. You know? She wasn't a bad person." It sounds ridiculous, even to me, but it's important to say.

"I know she wasn't," says the detective kindly. "Thank you, Ms. Donovan—Rain."

My mom shows him out. Then she sits down next to me and gives me a hug. "I'm proud of you, honey. I know that was not easy."

I smile. But I know: I didn't do anything.

DAY THREE

I'm so sorry.

I'm so sorry.

. . . so. Sorry.

God, Ms. Geller, I am . . .

There's no way, I think on the morning of Wendy's funeral. No way I will be able to say the right thing to Ms. Geller. Because there is no right thing to say.

There's a full-length mirror on the front of my closet door. I turn, examine myself.

A nice black suit—my mother says everyone should have one. Skirt almost to the knee, jacket fitted. Black shoes, heel not too high. Red hair, twisted up and out of sight. Pinky-beige lips, not terrible. Brown eyes, not terrible, except . . . brown. Pale face, rounder and fuller than I'd like. Body, same. Thin people look like they do things. Soft people look like they listen.

God, girl, I hear Wendy say. You look like you're going to a funeral.

I go to my bureau, take out my best chopsticks. Black and red with gold tips. Gently, I slide them into my hair. Then I ring my mouth with lipstick.

Better, Wen?

Better. Except, oops, still going to a funeral. What's up with that?

I don't know, Wendy. I don't know.

I'm sorry, Ms. Geller. I am so sorry.

Wendy was murdered early Sunday morning. She will be buried today. Before the burial, people are invited to give their condolences to the family at the Riverside Memorial Chapel. This won't be a funeral where a priest or rabbi talks and people say prayers—all that will happen later at the gravesite with just the family. Today will be more like a wake or shiva; people come and say how sorry they are and the family pretends it makes them feel better.

That afternoon, I take a cab to the funeral home. Taylor is meeting me there.

What can I do? I think as we sit in traffic. What right thing so that I don't say the horribly wrong thing?

I can say something not completely stupid to Wendy's mom.

Be there for Jenny Zalgat if she needs me.

Ellis. Definitely say something nice to Ellis.

Will Nico come? Can't imagine it. Probably he wants everyone to forget he ever knew Wendy.

I hear the cabdriver say, "This it?"

I look out the window. There are a lot of people outside. And cameras.

"This is that girl," says the driver. "The one in the park?"

"Her name was Wendy," I say, handing him the money and getting out.

Cruelly, it's a beautiful day. The gray clouds of November have cleared and the sky is bright blue overhead. The air is sharp and clear, but not too cold. It's a day to walk for miles, think big ideas, and dream of the future—not attend a funeral.

I've passed by Riverside a hundred times, but I've never been inside. It's a pretty building of red stone and granite. A square brown awning stands above the entrance. The big heavy doors have curtains over the glass. No peeking inside. Real life happening in here. And real death. As I wander through the crowd outside, I spot Taylor by the doors. Seeing her, I feel a rush of gratitude. Taylor didn't like Wendy, but she knows Wendy was my friend.

Taylor's hand on my arm. "Okay?"

I swallow. "No—but yeah."

We go through the doors and into what looks like the lobby of a cheesy hotel. Gilt and mirrors everywhere you look. Old-fashioned lights with plastic candles on the walls. Standing on an easel, a sign with the name *Geller* and a room number. This isn't about judgment or life or death. Now I feel like I'm at a wedding or bar mitzvah.

In a low voice, Taylor asks, "Is she here?"

"Who?"

"Wendy. Is . . . she here?" She doesn't want to say the word *body*. "Just sometimes they do open-casket. So, be ready for that."

No, I think. Not ready. There is no way I could be ready for such a thing. Why would you do that? I wonder, feeling panicked. Why would people want to see?

A small sign with gold letters tells us that Rooms A through D are to the left. Wendy is Room B. We go down a narrow hall. There's a long line to get into the room the Geller family has taken; I wonder if they knew there would be this many people. The walls are wood-paneled on the bottom, cream paper on the top. No windows, and I suck air, just to make sure I can. The carpet is thick, so no sound as you go, almost as if you don't exist. You're a ghost, entering a place between life and death, where everyone becomes a shadow.

As we finally make our way in, a man in a dark suit bows slightly and says, "Would you like to sign the book?"

Book? For a crazy moment, I think, Welcome to the afterlife. Please sign the Book of the Dead.

Taylor glances at me. I will have to go first. Stepping up, I find a leather book with a lovely pen resting in the spine. And lots of names. Some neat and tiny, some scrawled and rolling. Some are so small you can't read them, some so big you know whoever wrote them thought, Oh, I have the whole page.

I stare at them, trying to decipher the loops and lines. There, straight, small, precise, is *Ellis Patel.* Below his, in plump, friendly swirls, *Lindsey Adams.* Messy, jagged script—hurried, uncomfortable—*Karina Burroughs.* Two names in handwriting from another century: *Emile Dorland* and *Emily Laredo.*

I can't help it. I scan for Nico's name. I don't see it. Maybe he's on another page. I thumb the pages, wanting to look, but behind me I feel pressing, impatience. Taylor shifts nervously. I'm holding up the line. Quickly, I take the pen, write *Rain Donovan.* There are no lines on the page, so my name slopes down, looks like it's falling off a cliff. I hand the pen to Taylor, move away quickly.

Then I see the coffin. So much bigger than I expected. And brighter. Made of honey-brown wood—like violins, I think stupidly—it's the brightest thing in this horrible room. Small brass handles on the side. The top is open. I can see Wendy's hair.

I make a little noise, and immediately smack my hand to my mouth. Nobody needs to hear me cry.

I gather myself, crossing my arms tight around my middle, hands gripping my elbows. The room is ugly, I think fiercely. Red, white, and gold, the furniture overfussy, but cheap—so if someone spills, you can clean it easily. I hate the ugliness of this room.

Slowly, Taylor and I make our way through the crowd to a table where water, juice, and coffee are set up. Coffee and water are something to do. Safety. Taylor pours coffee into a plastic cup. I open a bottle of water.

"Is that her mom?" whispers Taylor, sipping.

I look where she's looking. A row of chairs. The family row. Ms. Geller is in the center, wearing a perfect black suit. Her back is straight, her chin up. Hands tight in her lap. Another woman—I'm guessing Wendy's aunt—sits near her. People approach in a steady stream, but they don't stay long. I see why. Ms. Geller radiates rage. Like the sun, her emotions are too intense to gaze at. You have to look away.

I'm so sorry, Ms. Geller, so sorry.

Who cares if you're sorry? I imagine her screaming at me. How does sorry help my daughter?

Taylor asks, "Is it Ms. Geller or something else?"

"Geller. She built up her real estate business with it, so she wanted to keep the name." Wendy always said it made her mom a hypocrite. "Oh, yeah, dump him, but keep his name—nice."

"Is that Wendy's dad?" whispers Taylor, pointing to a tall gray-haired man. He's surrounded by people, chatting away as if he's at a cocktail party. Disliking him, I remember Wendy saying, My dad? Oh, you're like the most important person in his life. For the five whole seconds he notices you.

Next to him is a younger woman, also in a black suit, but

somehow it makes her look like a kid. She has long blond hair and keeps licking her lips nervously. Her eyes dart around the room. When someone speaks to her, she nods too quickly, says "Um-hm" a lot.

Gee, Dad, trophy wife, how freakin' original. I mean, couldn't you at least pick one with a brain?

"And stepmother," I whisper. "Heidi, I think." This is better. Standing on the side, figuring out the who's who.

"Let me guess," says Taylor. "Wendy hated her."

"Not her favorite," I say, smiling. In a weird way, talking about the drama of Wendy's life—Wendy's favorite subject—makes her seem still alive.

I point out Wendy's aunt, who gave the statement to the newspaper, then a cousin and maybe an uncle. A few couples look slightly out of place; Long Island friends and neighbors, I would guess. Under the "I'm so sorrys" and the "So terribles," you hear murmurs of "the guy." "The crazy." The one who's still out there.

I see teachers. Ms. Marengi, who teaches math at Alcott, and Mr. Alexandrov, who does history. I look for Mr. Farrell, feel a thud of disappointment that he's not here.

I hear Taylor say, "There's Karina."

I see Karina talking with Amy Charteris. Instinctively, I look for Nico; if he's here, he'll be near this crew.

While I'm searching, Mr. Alexandrov, who's the advisor for the newspaper, comes up to Taylor. Taylor starts complaining about Dorland's censorship. For a few minutes, I stand awkwardly, pretending I'm part of their conversation. But Taylor won't stop talking until she gets the change she wants or she gets tired, which could take quite a while.

Edging toward the window, I think, I should be able to do this. Be alone in a group. Taylor does not have to take care of me. I can nod, say hi. Possibly even have a conversation. Although, what do you talk about? "Wow, Wendy's dead, that's horrible." "Yeah, totally sucks. Hey—did you do the reading for English?"

What would Wendy do? I ask myself. If this were her, and I was the one who was dead?

Well, I realize, she wouldn't be standing in a corner, terrified to make eye contact. She wouldn't be hiding from my mom. Wendy would plop herself right down next to my mom, give her one of those big hugs, and come up with ten amazing things to say about me.

Or she'd find some cute guy and flirt with him. But she wouldn't be hiding. She wouldn't be scared.

Making a decision, I raise my head. Eyes now available for contact!

And who do I make eye contact with? Karina. Great.

She's several people away from me—on her own, which gives me a certain bitchy satisfaction as I remember all the times she chanted Rain, Rain, go away. DON'T come back another day.

I smile vaguely, expecting a dismissive eye roll in return. But instead, she gives me a small wave.

And then actually starts making her way toward me.

Amazed, I wonder, did Karina overmedicate this morning? Has the funeral parlor formaldehyde gone to her head? But before I can deal with the utter bizarreness of a friendly Karina, I hear a moan of sorrow. Turning, I can see Jenny Zalgat through the crowd. Her hand is pressed hard to her mouth. Her knees are folding. Her eyes are fixed on the coffin.

Karina can wait. I push through the crowd, grab Jenny's free hand. Thinking of Wendy's hugs, I hold it hard. Jenny clings on to me, her eyes still on the coffin.

I whisper, "You want to say good-bye?"

Her hand tightens on mine. She nods again.

As we move toward Wendy, I think how much easier this is with Jenny here. Jenny can be the one who's scared. I'll be the one who's calm. I take a deep breath. Look down.

What I see is not Wendy. It's a bad doll someone clumped together with clay and paint, using some old photo of Wendy bored out of her mind at a family event. Wendy's hair is brushed in a way she never wore it, high and off her forehead. The hands on her chest look like wax. There's beige makeup smeared all over her face. The lipstick's too red, the eye shadow too dark. Someone put her in a black dress with a cardigan. There's a scarf around her neck, an ugly green thing.

"Okay," I hear Jenny whisper, "what she would say if she could? 'Get these ugly-ass clothes off me.'"

I have to press my lips together to keep from laughing, because it's so true and it's so good to think of Wendy saying that. It's stupid—who cares what you wear when you're dead?—but appearance was important to Wendy.

Then I see the bruises. Dark shadows under the thick yellow paste. One high on her cheek, near the eye. Another on her chin. And, just visible at the edge of the scarf, the stain of death on her throat.

I hear Jenny's choked whisper. "Bye, sweetie." But I'm not saying good-bye. Not to this, because this is not Wendy. I don't know if there's a God or heaven, but there are spirits. A you-ness, a life. But it's not here in this box. This is just some old clothes.

I don't want to stand here staring. I have to do something, something good. My list. Useless, but all I have. Say something nice to Ms. Geller. Do what Wendy would have done for my mom. The crowd around her has cleared. A dark-haired boy sits beside her, doubled over.

Ellis.

Be kind to Ellis, another thing I meant to do. Good, two things at once.

But as I approach, I suddenly feel like an intruder. Trying to sense where it's coming from, I look to Ms. Geller. But her back's to me, she's not even aware I'm near. It's Ellis. As he talks to her, he keeps glancing at me. We know each other slightly, but there's no recognition in his eyes. No welcome.

He doesn't want me, I think. I should back off.

But that's what I always think. Rain, I tell myself—for once, don't listen. Just say what you should.

I say, "Ms. Geller? Rain . . ."

"Oh, Rain." She gets up immediately. Hugs me. "Thank you for coming."

"Of course."

"I'm so sorry," I hear myself say.

Ms. Geller squeezes my hands. "I know." Her voice shudders as she says, "She was my sweet, funny baby."

I nod, feeling choked up. "She was . . ."

God, why can I never say things?

Ellis stands and—maybe to rescue me—Ms. Geller asks, "Rain, do you know Wendy's boyfriend, Ellis?"

Boyfriend? I hug Ellis, say, "Yeah, sure. Hi."

He hugs back, but steps away quickly. I didn't read him wrong before. He doesn't want me here.

Jolted, I focus on his clothes. Ellis has fun with his clothes, he and Wendy had that in common. His suit is dark navy. His shirt is clean, simple white, with a dark-gray tie of heavy silk. Even in mourning, Ellis dresses well. Wendy would like that, I think.

Then Ms. Geller says, "Rain and Wendy were good friends when they were younger." She manages a shaky smile. "You two had some adventures."

Well, not actually the two of us, I think, remembering how Wendy used me to cover. I try to joke. "You weren't supposed to know that."

Ellis smiles nervously. Wanting to signal that I'm not out to embarrass him, I say, "You and Wendy were so great together."

He manages to nod thank you, then says, "She was amazing."

Ms. Geller puts her hand on Ellis's arm. "Ellis was such an important part of Wendy's life. We're so happy to have him as . . . well, I think of you as family. I do."

We all smile. Then Ellis's mouth twists and he tears up again. Ms. Geller murmurs, "Oh," and hugs him. While I think, Chill out. You dated for, like, six weeks.

Putting the thought away, I say to Ms. Geller, "I know everybody says this, but if there's anything . . ."

The squeeze again, the smile. "Thank you. I always knew my girl was in good hands with you."

My throat tightens as I feel again how much I let Wendy down. "Well, I'll let you . . ."

What? Cry? Scream?

Ms. Geller gives me a quick hug, then lets me go.

Making my way back through the crowd, I see Lindsey Adams. She's standing by a large, ugly plant, arms crossed, staring at nothing. I remember now: she and Ellis had some girlfriend vs. friend issues while he was with Wendy. This can't be fun for her. I wave, but she seems determined not to see anyone.

Wiggling through the crowd, I hear snatches of conversation. "My niece was attacked walking her dog." "You walk down the street, you don't know what's coming at you." "I bet they never catch him."

I find Taylor chatting with a stranger. But the second she sees me, she says to the woman, "Again—I'm really sorry." Taylor can do it, I think enviously. Sound grown-up and sincere even with someone she just met.

"Who was that?" I ask as we walk away.

"Long Island neighbor. Said she worried about Wendy moving to the city. You know, 'with all the psychos.'" Taylor rolls her eyes. "I need to know what a bathroom looks like in a funeral home. You?"

"No, I'm good." Taylor nods, heads off to one of the men in black to ask directions.

Waiting, I wander the lobby. There are other signs, other names, other rooms. How many dead people are here? I wonder. Then, How many people have died today? How many are buried, graves like craters all over the earth? I imagine the earth crumbling under so many dead.

Behind me, I hear, "Hey."

I turn, see Karina. "Hey."

Both heys are wary. We don't like each other and we know it. Yet here we are.

Karina says, "Pretty awful, huh." She could be talking about the decor. But I'll decide she means Wendy.

"Horrible," I say, even as I keep track of how many words I'm saying. "I'll miss her."

"Yeah"—her voice quickens, I just gave her an opening—"I saw you talking to her at the party."

I nod as I take in this clue to the mystery of Karina's sudden friendliness.

She asks, "Have you done the police talk?"

Done the police talk—Karina makes it sound like a joke. Boring, like homework. "Yeah. I didn't have anything to tell them."

Karina nods, trying to be sympathetic. "I told them how worried I was about her that night. It's one thing if you go after a guy and bomb out in private. But to tell the whole world? Humiliate yourself like that? I mean . . . no wonder, right?"

No wonder she ended up murdered? Because she liked a boy? Don't quite get the connection there, Karina.

Unless you want to tell me that the boy she liked murdered her.

Do I remember that Karina dated Nico a long time ago? Or am I making that up?

Then Karina asks, "What were you guys talking about?"

Her eyes are right on me. This is not a casual question.

"Um . . . party talk," I say carefully. "'Hey, how are you?' That kind of thing."

"Really? You guys were chatting for a while."

Now I want to know. Whatever it is Karina's fishing for, I want to know what it is—and why. Which means risking just a little more.

Shrugging, I say, "Just life, love, pursuit of happiness kind of things." I slow down over the s's, try to get them right. Once

Karina spent a whole lunch hour shushing everyone whenever I said an s. "Sh, everybody! Rain says shush, be quiet."

But if my s's aren't perfect, Karina doesn't seem to notice today. "She was talking about Nico, right?" She rolls her eyes, inviting me into her club briefly to make fun of Wendy.

"A little."

Karina smirks. "What, she was all like, 'Oh, he's totally going home with me'?"

One thing Karina is telling me without saying a word: she's worried people will think Wendy got with Nico. That's why she wants to know what Wendy said to people that night.

She's also told me I'm not the only one who's connected the question mark around Nico and Wendy with Wendy's death.

Karina presses. "That's the thing, she told everyone. Put it on her stupid Facebook page. Then when it didn't happen, she couldn't handle it."

One of the things that has worked for me in the past: be the nerd who knows nothing. Frowning, I say, "Oh, it didn't happen? Her and Nico? 'Cause I heard—"

I break off, as if confused.

"What?" Anger now, narrowing her eyes, flushing her cheeks. "Someone's saying they left together? Because they didn't. No way."

"No, the person didn't say that—"

Karina interrupts. "Is this Jenny? Chick's off her meds. I saw Wendy leave. And believe me, she was all on her lonesome."

She makes a fake sad face, her contempt for Wendy right out there. The need to do something that I felt looking into Wendy's coffin floods back. And with it an idea. Usually, I don't lie well. But now I need to.

My voice vague, I say, "Yeah, but you know what's funny? I was waiting for a cab. And I could have sworn I saw Nico outside."

My heart pounds as I wait for Karina to call me a liar or say she has no idea what I'm talking about. But as Karina stays silent, the pounding starts to feel like: You're right. You're right. You're right.

She steps in close. "If I were you, I would not be spreading that around. Nico only left to—"

Then she realizes what she's admitted.

"Stay out of it," she hisses. "This is real life, okay? You don't know shit." She leans down, whispers, "Keep your mouth shut, Rain. It's the only time people can stand to be around you."

For a moment, I wonder, Is that true? But I sense Karina's fear, and that gives me the strength to say, "Well, here's what I know, Karina. I know Nico left the party. And I know you're worried about it. And that's a lot. Thanks."

Then I leave before she can say another word.

When Taylor comes out on the street, she sees my face and says, "What? What happened?"

"I can't here," I tell her. "Let's walk."

We head uptown, moving through the bright normal world of Amsterdam Avenue. There are moms pushing strollers toward the park, little kids coming home from school. Someone's going into Starbucks, another into a dry cleaner's.

Then Taylor stops. "Okay, it's far enough. Speak."

I lower my voice, "Karina just told me Nico left with Wendy that night."

"But he didn't," says Taylor with maddening certainty.

"Okay, like right after Wendy."

"And?"

I widen my eyes. "And? That means—at the very least—he was the last person to see her alive."

"You absolutely do not know that."

"Tay . . ."

"He could have left to get booze, cigarettes, a breath of fresh air."

"Or be with Wendy."

Taylor shrugs.

"Why do you think that's so impossible?"

Taylor sighs. "Because if he did it, he'd be arrested by now. Besides, he's with Sasha, and Wendy was a skank."

I wince. "Jesus, Tay."

"I'm sorry." She puts an awkward hand on my arm. I shake it off. "But just because Wendy made up this whole story about how she was going to get Nico—doesn't make it so."

"Why are you taking his side?"

"I'm not. It just pisses me off that because of what Wendy said, you think this guy killed her."

"I do not think that."

"Don't you?" She challenges me with her eyes.

For a moment, I think of stepping down, saying, You're right, I'm nuts. What am I thinking?

Then I remember what I'm thinking. I'm thinking Nico's sneer, his finger jamming into my mouth. I'm thinking Karina's fear. How everyone wants to say how screwed up Wendy was, but no one says how screwed up Nico is.

"Why don't you think it?" I snap. "At all? Why is it so impossible to think?"

Taylor doesn't answer.

Frustrated, I say, "Tell me what you're thinking."

Taylor stares down the block. "I'm just wondering . . ."

"What?"

"I know people were pretty crappy to you about the whole speech thing. I don't know if Nico ever . . ."

"No." I see where Taylor's going and I don't want to give her any ammunition.

"But people like him—the Karinas of this world—they can be . . ."

"Evil," I say simply.

Taylor nods reluctantly. "So, I don't blame you for hating them. At all. But I'm not going to make the jump to murder, either. Because what I saw is Wendy leaving alone." She hesitates. "And I swear I saw Nico at the party when I left."

That throws me. But then I say, "He did it and came back."

"The guy really didn't look like he killed somebody," says Taylor. "I'm sorry, sweetie. Look, if you're right, I'm sure the police are on it."

But how can the police be on it when Nico's friends are protecting him? Who's going to say he left the party? Not Karina. Not Sasha. I even protected him, I realize. I didn't tell them half the things I could have.

Then Taylor says, "But just so you know, I did tell the cops I saw Nico at the party when I left."

"What else did they want to know?"

She rolls her eyes. "Was I at the party? Did I know Wendy? What'd I think about how she seemed that night?"

"What'd you tell them?"

"What I told you. That she seemed crazed and she didn't have a habit of making the best choices. I'm sorry, that's what I saw."

"It's okay," I say, numb and automatic.

"We good?" Her voice is uncertain.

I don't want to fight with Taylor, so I say, "Yeah, sure."

There's an awkward silence. Trying to ease it, Taylor says, "Cops are so obvious, the way they try and put you at ease. They were like, 'Oh, we hear you're the coeditor of the school newspaper. Big achiever. Got an *E* pin.'"

Puzzled, I say, "How'd they know? They saw it on your bag?"

She shakes her head. "I didn't have it with me. Who knows? They're goons." She gives me a hug. "I'm really sorry, Rain," she whispers. "You don't deserve this pain."

Then she nods toward the crosstown bus stop. "I'm going to get this. See you tomorrow."

I nod.

As I walk home, the heels hurt my feet and I don't care because I'm so angry. Skank, bitch, slut—everyone talks about Wendy like she was some trashy whore who made yet another mistake. While Nico's just fine. People are excusing him, covering for him, just like they always have.

Do you really think he killed Wendy? a voice whispers.

I don't know, I answer. But I want to know why he left the party right after her.

That's not proof of anything, the voice insists.

And that, I have to admit, is true. Still, I wonder, do the police know Nico left the party?

Should I tell them?

On the corner, I'm stopped short by the sight of Wendy's face.

Smiling, pretty, but grainy, out of focus. Because it's printed on cheap paper, the kind you toss away when you're done. Wendy's on the front page of the *Herald*. Above her face, crowding it, the words . . .

WHO WAS WENDY GELLER?
Life of a Party Girl Ends in Violence

Snatching up the paper, I put a dollar on the counter and don't wait for change. I fold the newspaper under my arm and head to the nearest Starbucks. It's packed with Columbia kids, but I find a stool in the corner and start to read.

Wendy Geller's young life came to a tragic end early Sunday morning. Her body was found beaten and strangled in Central Park. How did a wealthy, popular girl, who attended one of the city's finest schools, end up dead and thrown away like so much trash? The answer may lie with today's hard-partying teens—kids with too much money and not enough guidance from permissive moms and dads who want to be their kids' friends instead of their parents.

Seventeen-year-old Wendy was pretty, outgoing, and popular. The stylish teenager had many friends at the prestigious Alcott School in Manhattan. But she also made enemies.

"She'd get in fights with other girls," said one Alcott student. "Over stupid stuff. Like they hadn't invited her to a party or said something behind her back. She'd get revenge by messing around with their boyfriends."

Wendy reportedly kept a "hit list" in her diaries and later on her Facebook page. In the list, she kept a record of boys she was interested in. Generally, they were already dating other people.

"Nobody will say this," said the student, "but there are some people here who aren't too sad to see her go. Like, not that she deserved it. But—karma, you know?"

Sources say that Geller had attended a party the night she was murdered. Toxicology reports have not come back yet, but witnesses report that Geller was "trashed."

"She had on her little happy high," said one source.

Taylor, I think, oh my God. They're quoting Taylor. That reporter in the diner yesterday—she must have overheard our conversation.

The city has seen many young women's lives end in violence. Young women who court danger and find it. One wonders if their parents know—or care—what they're doing.

"Sadly," said a source close to the investigation, "there are instances when young women indulge in drugs and alcohol . . ."

Who says Wendy took drugs? I wonder furiously. Nobody, nobody said that.

"They're walking around, not in the best state to make good decisions, and tragically, it ends like this."

I can't believe it. All anyone can talk about is Wendy—as if she somehow did this to herself. I look at the name on the article. Stella Walcott. Digging in my book bag, I find that card.

Stella Walcott.

Speak for her, speak for Wendy.

Yeah, I think, maybe I should.

Sitting on the stone wall by Central Park, I dial Stella Walcott's number. As the phone starts to ring, a voice whispers, You're leaving yourself wide open. She's smarter than you. Crueler. You think you're defending Wendy, but she'll turn it into something ugly.

Help Wendy, I tell myself firmly.

"Stella Walcott."

I'm startled by Stella's actual voice. She sounds normal, friendly, and for a moment, I feel my anger melt. Then I see two girls walk by. They're laughing, heads together. In a flash, I remember Gillian Lasker, the flushing sound. Everyone judging Wendy, deciding who she was.

"Party girl," I say harshly.

"Excuse me?"

"I didn't say that. I would never call Wendy a party girl. Or any cutesy nickname."

There's a little pause. Then: "Who is this?"

"How about Diner Girl?"

"The one with the attitude or the one with the chopsticks?"

"Chopsticks."

"Well, hello. I thought you had something to say." Her voice is warmer now. You may hate me, but I'm liking you a lot.

It makes me feel disgusting. Like getting groped by some pervert on the street.

"Did you go to the service? What was it like?"

Ignoring her questions, I tell her, "Yeah, here's what I have to say. You suck. Oh, and also, get your facts right."

"Tell me where I got it wrong."

Her tone tells me I can do this. I can set the story straight. She will listen to me.

This is a trap, my fear whispers.

"Drugs," I say. "We never said she did drugs."

"I got that from another source."

"Who?"

"Would you want me to tell people where I got 'trashed' from?"

No, I think. I feel defeated. Let's face it. Wendy was trashed. Wendy probably did do drugs. Wendy was a party girl.

I struggle to pull Wendy out of the tangle of gossip and headlines, to remember what it felt like to be with her.

"What'd I get wrong?" Stella presses. "What'd I leave out?"

The dough rocks raw, am I right?

Speak up, girl!

I hear Wendy's laugh, the hoarseness of her voice as she said "Uuuggghhh" whenever there was something she didn't want to do, the way she made you feel like you were the most amazing person she'd ever known.

"Wendy," I say flatly. "You left Wendy out. You got her way, way wrong. She cared about people. I'm not saying she was some saint. But she wasn't all about herself." I think of Jenny sobbing in the hallway. "She was a good friend." I think of Ellis. "People loved her. Her mom loved her. And she loved them back. Sometimes too much, and she got hurt. And now someone's"—I can't say it—"and you're acting like she's some idiot who was in the park to score drugs and got what she deserved."

There's a long pause. Then Stella says, "You really care about this girl."

Not enough, I think, when it mattered. "Everybody screws up, you know?"

"Yeah, I do know," says Stella. "We all have our crazy years. Lord knows I had mine."

Her voice is wistful. In the quiet, I like her.

Then she asks, "Seriously. Can you tell me what Wendy was doing in the park?"

"I can't. I wish I knew."

There's another pause. "I have another question for you, but I need to know you can keep a secret. Can you?"

My heart leaps. They know who killed Wendy. Stella's going to tell me. "Sure."

"Does *E* mean anything to you?"

"*E*," I repeat, confused. *E* is not a name. *E* is not . . .

Then in a flash, I see Sasha's hand as she brushes her hair, the *E*, gold and black, on her finger.

Answer a question with a question. "Why?"

I hear a sigh. Not giving up, deciding. "Look. I'm going to let you in on something the rest of the city isn't going to know for a few days. That's a big deal in my world."

"Mine too," I say. "I'm in high school."

A short laugh. "So, you understand what I'm saying. Sometimes I go drinking with a guy who works as a guard in an evidence room. You know what that is?"

Remembering my mom's *Law & Order* obsession, I say, "Where cops store the evidence in an investigation?"

"Right. And he happens to work the precinct that's handling this particular case. They logged an item they found at the scene. But they're not telling anyone about it."

"Why not?"

"Who knows? A lot of the time, they hold back a piece of evidence to weed out fake suspects, people who might lie and say they killed Wendy just for kicks."

"Was it a pin or—"

"No details. What I want to know is, did it belong to Wendy?"

No, I think. No, no, no. Wendy was not the kind of girl to get an E. Ever.

Which means . . .

It belongs to Wendy's killer.

Stella presses. "Come on, Rain. If it's not Wendy's, whose is it? Who is E, Rain?"

Not who, I think, what. But I'm not telling Stella that.

Wendy's killer is not some random crazy person. He's someone I've passed in the halls. Someone I've spoken to.

I know Wendy's killer.

DAY FOUR

The next morning, I get to school early. I walk through the quiet halls, passing through the strips of sunlight that beam in from the windows. It is very precise light. One step, sun, warmth. Next step, dark, chill.

Last night, I reminded myself that an E pin near Wendy doesn't actually prove someone from school killed her. Some kid could have dropped it walking home. It could have been there for months.

Girlfriends and boyfriends give each other E pins. Ellis could have one. Maybe he gave it to Wendy and didn't ask for it back. She was wearing it the night she was killed, and it got pulled off in the struggle.

Then I remembered that Mr. Dorland once said that there are fewer than five hundred E pins in the whole world. The school only gives out four a year. People take them seriously. They don't tend to lose them. And even if Ellis did give her a pin, Wendy would have given it back the second she broke up with him. There's no way she would have kept it.

Which means there aren't a million reasons the pin could have been there. Not thousands of people who could have left it near Wendy's body. There aren't even a hundred.

There's only one. The person who killed her.

But would Nico have had an E pin?

It seems highly unlikely. He's been a slacker ever since he got to Alcott. But Oliver Travers was also a slacker; just his parents happened to donate an organic greenhouse to the school.

That's why I have to find out for sure.

The library is one of my favorite places at school. It takes up two floors, with circular stairwells that lead to the second level. Other parts of the school have been modernized since my mom went here, but not the library. It still has the dark wood tables with green-shaded reading lights. Huge iron chandeliers hang from the ceiling, stained-glass philosophers and saints beam colored sun spots all around the hall. There are computers, but they're kept in a separate room. This is a cathedral for books. Stacks and stacks of books with knowledge dating back to the beginning of time.

Normally, I like to sit at a table right near the big picture window that looks out onto Riverside Park. But this morning, I head upstairs to an aisle far in the back where no one ever goes except to text or make out. This is where they keep the books that haven't been touched in years, the kinds of things that went onto computers ages ago. Encyclopedias. Dictionaries.

And the yearbooks. One for every year, going back to 1924, when the school was founded.

The list of new E pin recipients is printed in the yearbook. No other announcement is ever made, and it's understood that you're not supposed to ask. The way you find out someone got one is if you read that page in the yearbook or you see them wearing it. *If* you see them wearing it. Generally you don't know who has an E pin. Unless you make a point of finding out.

I sit down cross-legged, pull out the book from my freshman

year. Fascinated by the faces, I take my time. It's only two years ago, and already, people look different. Finding the page with Ms. Epstein's homeroom, I see Wendy, her arms wrapped around Jenny Zalgat. Heads together, like sisters. Karina's in the back row with some friends—flashing teeth, arms out like showgirls. I hadn't remembered she and Wendy were in the same homeroom that year.

I turn the page, find my homeroom, Ms. Phillipousis. When they took this picture, I was no longer friends with Wendy.

Steeling myself, I look closer. I am standing alone at the edge of the group. I am wrapped in my army jacket, hands in my pockets. My hair is long, parted down the middle. No chopsticks or combs. I am very serious about not looking trivial in any way. I am refusing to smile.

Rain, Rain, go away . . .

I try to remember. Was I really that pissed off? I just remember feeling sad.

Next is Mr. Chen's homeroom. Ellis, in full goofball mode, mugging for the camera. No Lindsey—she must have been in another class. I turn the page. Here she is. Short and stocky, but a very pretty face, with brown curls. She's cut them since this picture was taken. She looks girly here. And prettier, I guess. But she looks better now.

And here's Sasha, ravishing even in the tenth grade. Unlike a lot of girls, she strikes no pose. She doesn't need to.

Turn the page. Nico's homeroom. Nico—beautiful and pouting in the back row. A boring model wannabe. Obnoxious, but harmless. We choose how we list our names. Nico chose *Nicholas Andrew Phelps,* like he's some WASP god.

This boy does not have an E pin, I think. No way.

But Sasha does, a voice whispers.

Which I know because I saw her wearing it. So—obviously she didn't give it to Nico.

I look again at Nico's picture. See arrogance, selfishness.

And anger.

Unnerved, I turn the page.

Ah, sigh, Mr. Farrell's class. His first year here, standing straight and solemn beside his students. I smile, brush his image with my finger.

Okay, turn the page, Rain.

Our School! Candid shots. Lots of pictures of Nico; I wonder if he was dating someone on the yearbook staff. All the images have the same poseyness. He's got the right clothes, the right hair. But to me, he looks out of place, as if secretly, he hates everybody's guts.

I hit the senior section, kids long gone now from Alcott. Photos, quotes from songs, poetry, books, Einstein, Che, Dorothy Parker. Everyone trying to be cool or deep or smart. So weird, how we use someone else's words to say who we are.

At the end of the senior pages, I find what I came for: the honors lists. I scan all the awards to the someone most promising at something. Turning the page, I see in small, gray type . . .

This year's recipients of the E Pin

I read the names.

Henry Abelard
Peter Dorkey
Anya Kwiatkowski
Sasha Meloni

Henry and Anya have graduated. Henry is Taylor's brother, and he wasn't aware Wendy existed, as far as I know. Peter's a sweetheart who, despite being a hundred pounds overweight, gets the lead in the school musical every year. He has no connection to Wendy that I can think of.

I reach for last year's yearbook, go straight to the back of the book.

This year's recipients of the E Pin
Oliver Travers
Lorelei Haneke
Sasha Meloni
Taylor Abelard

Oliver graduated. Lorelei uses a wheelchair. One E pin for Taylor. Two for Sasha.

But none for Ellis. Which means it couldn't have been his E pin they found near Wendy. He didn't have one to give her.

And as I thought, none for Nico.

But Sasha has two. Which means . . . what, exactly? Can she be that serious about Nico? That she would give him an E pin?

The names of the E pin recipients seem to lift off the page, floating before my eyes, making me dizzy.

"Hiding?" I look up, see—oh my God—Mr. Farrell.

Shutting the yearbook, I say, "Um, yes. Always."

He smiles. Waits a moment.

Then he says, "I just came in early to do some research. I didn't mean to interrupt. . . ."

I glance at the yearbook, then at Mr. Farrell. It's like taking your first step into the murky, silty part of the pond where the water's muddy, the bottom's slippery, and you don't know what you'll step on.

"Mr. Farrell?" I say it quickly before I have time to think.

"Yes?"

"Can we talk?"

This is wrong, I tell myself as we walk to Mr. Farrell's room. But sometimes the wrong thing is the only thing you can do. A very Wendy thing to think, I realize. But Mr. Farrell really is the one person who might take me seriously—but not so seriously that he would tell me I have to go to the police.

He shuts the door after me, sits, and pulls out a chair next to his. I think: If he hated that I like him, he would not do these things.

I sit. Have no idea how to start.

Mr. Farrell, I think Nico Phelps might have killed Wendy.

That's very nice, Rain. Give me a sec, I need to call Mental Health Services.

Then I hear Mr. Farrell ask, "Did you go to the service?"

"Yes."

He waits for a moment. "And?"

"It was . . ." I didn't come here to talk about the coffin. How Wendy looked. Because if I talk about those things, I will start crying.

"It was sad. I've never been to one before."

"I'm so sorry that was your first one," Mr. Farrell says. "I can't imagine."

"Yeah." I smile. "I hope they get better—if that makes any sense."

He thinks for a long moment, then says softly, "I think they'll feel less unfair."

Unfair—it's the right word. I feel teary, look down. After a moment, I hear him say, "Take your time."

"No." I have this together, I do. "Actually, I have this other thing I wanted to talk about." His brows come together: nervous. He doesn't want to be a sponge for teenage blah blah.

"It's about Wendy," I assure him. "It's just hard to say."

"Nothing about this is easy." There's a little laugh at the end that breaks the spell.

Folding my arms, I sit back. "I've been thinking about who did this."

He waits.

"And—warning, this is going to sound insane. . . ."

He smiles. I smile back. Try to think how to start.

There is no start. Just say it.

"I think someone from school might have killed Wendy."

Mr. Farrell just stares at me. He takes a deep breath in. Breathing out, he says, "Okay."

He is shocked. A little afraid. "It's something you feel or—?"

"Sort of." Coughing slightly, I say, "I don't know how much you knew about Wendy. . . ."

"I knew her from my class, of course. Outside of that . . ." He shakes his head.

"Well . . ." I want to tell the truth but not meanly. "Wendy would get obsessed with certain guys."

It's too weird, talking about guys with Mr. Farrell, so I blurt out, "I mean, I don't know if you know about the whole Facebook thing, how Wendy was always talking about this guy. . . ."

He's utterly confused now. Trying to start over, I say, "Wendy really liked this boy and she wanted to . . ."

"She wanted his attention," says Mr. Farrell politely.

"Yes," I say gratefully. "And she told everybody she was going to get it at this party."

"The party she went to on the night she died."

I nod again.

"And did she get it?"

"I think she did," I say quietly. "I think he left the party and met her."

Mr. Farrell coughs a little, sits up. Now his arms are folded. Is he taking me seriously? Or is he about to kick me out? *Look, Rain, you can't come in here with these wild accusations.*

He says abruptly, "Let's be clear. I don't know much about students' lives outside class, but I do hear things. We're talking about Nico Phelps, right?"

It's a relief to have the name spoken and have nothing explode. "Yes."

"Have you talked to Detective Vasquez?"

"No."

"You need to."

His voice is firm. This is all moving too fast from my head to reality. "And say what? 'Uh, Officer, I think Nico Phelps killed Wendy Geller'? 'Gee, why?' ''Cause he left the party around the same time she did.'" I lift my hands as if to show Mr. Farrell how hopeless it is.

"Is that the only reason you suspect him?" asks Mr. Farrell.

"No." I so want to tell Mr. Farrell about the E pin. But Stella Walcott said the police wanted to keep it a secret. I cannot be responsible for screwing up the investigation into Wendy's death.

Mr. Farrell shoves his chair back. "I'm serious, Rain. This is not something for me to hear. It's for the police."

Panicked, I shake my head. "But I don't know anything for sure."

"Tell them what you do know."

What I do know. I try to sort the tangled threads that make up my feeling that Nico is guilty. Wendy telling Jenny, *Leave, split, I'm cool.* The ugly finger in my mouth, Karina's fear. But it's all just feeling. No facts—unless I can prove that Nico had an E pin. Maybe Sasha gave him one of hers, but I need to know that before I say anything. Well, anything more. Plus, I have to make sure all the other kids still have theirs. That their pins aren't sitting in an evidence locker.

Taylor's isn't, I think. One of Sasha's isn't.

Mr. Farrell settles back into his chair. "Rain, I know some of the kids are very upset that the police want to interview them. Sasha Meloni has refused to speak with them. Is it that you're scared?"

I nod.

"Of what?" he asks. "That people will be angry? That absurd 'no snitching' rule?"

The rule for some kids isn't no snitching, I want to tell Mr. Farrell. It's no talking. No being.

"Are you frightened of Nico?" he asks gently.

This is closer, and I nod. "Maybe it's just me. I know a lot of kids like him . . ."

Mr. Farrell threads his fingers together, focuses on the tight knot of his hands. "If I say something, Rain, do I have your promise you won't repeat it? I'm about to be very unprofessional."

"I promise," I whisper.

"Nico worries me. He has since he arrived at Alcott. There's an anger in him I find disturbing. He's a young man very much at odds with his surroundings, yet he's desperate to belong."

I nod.

Mr. Farrell says, "I don't wish to speak ill of him. But for many reasons, he doesn't belong at Alcott. He knows it, and it makes him feel inferior. Which makes him angry. I know he's had . . . incidents before this one."

Stealing from Daisy Loring. Throwing a drink in Kirsty Pennington's face. I want to tell Mr. Farrell about what Nico did to me, but I don't want to ask for pity.

He's waiting for me to say I'll do it, I realize. Go to the police, tell them what I suspect. But I can't. The thought of going to them, saying I know this! Put this person in jail! makes me sick.

He sighs; I hate the sound. It's disappointment. *Rain needs to participate more in class. . . .*

"Is there something that would be the proof you need, something you could find out?"

The E pin. "I think so."

"If you get it, that bit of proof you need—promise me you'll go to the police?"

I hesitate. "The cops would have talked to him, right? She made her thing for Nico pretty clear. She even put it on her Facebook page."

"Yes. They've talked to him. I gather they didn't get much." He sighs. "And there are a lot of kids who might be willing to lie for him. Or stay silent to protect him."

I can't argue with that. Even if Sasha did give him one of her pins, who would tell the police? Obviously not Sasha, if she won't even talk to them.

"This is probably all in my head," I say, half hoping he'll agree with me. "I just feel like there has to be something I can do for Wendy."

"Of course."

"So, I'm deciding"—I let sarcasm into my voice—"that I've found her killer."

"Or, you're dealing with a very angry young man who reacts to any threat with violence. And if that's what you're doing, I don't want you to be doing it alone."

He reaches for a notebook, then picks up a pen. He scribbles something, hands it to me.

"My phone number," he says. "If you're worried, nervous, think you've learned something—call. Okay?"

"Okay." I take the piece of paper, fold it carefully, and put it in my bag.

"Whatever you need." I look in his eyes and it's true. Whatever I need, this man will give me.

And as I look and keep looking, it becomes clear that what I might need is not so safe or easy; he sees that, but he's not looking away. For a brief moment, I'm not a kid and he's not a teacher.

Then Mr. Farrell stands up. The talk is over. I have to thank him, I think, as I agree to be led to the door. You have to say thank you when someone says they want to protect you.

"Just . . . talk to me," says Mr. Farrell. "Okay, Rain?"

He slides his hand down my arm.

Then he ducks his head, steps back awkwardly, and shuts the door.

It's nothing, I think. There's nothing wrong with it.

Yes, there is, I think breathlessly as I hurry down the hallway. Mr. Farrell touched me. He touched me, when he didn't want to, but he had to. And now he feels bad, and he wishes he hadn't done it. That's why he stepped back so fast, why he closed the door. Because he felt guilty.

But also thrilled.

Because that's how I feel and I know. I know he feels the same way. There are things I know, things I feel. And this is one of them. I dared to speak. And look what happened. For once, I am totally rewarded. Which may be a weird way to think about it, but that's how it feels.

Down the hall is Ms. Englander's classroom. She teaches World Civilization. Her walls are covered with images from the Bible, Greek mythology, and fairy tales. Passing by, I see Eve at the tree, Pandora, Bluebeard's wife. All those women in stories opening boxes they're not supposed to, peeking through doors to see what they shouldn't, eating forbidden fruit. They do it because they want to know what's really going on. They want to feel alive.

Why are they always told no?

But I have to be fair about this. Not jump to conclusions. First thing to do: account for all the other E pins. The kids who have graduated are off my list. I've seen one of Sasha's, I've seen Taylor's. Of the kids still at Alcott, that leaves Peter Dorkey and Lorelei Haneke.

I have chorus that morning. So, as it happens, does Peter. He sings bass. I've already told my mom she'll probably run into him at Lincoln Center one day. He's that good.

And a really good person. Always helps the new guys feel okay about singing in chorus by bellowing, "We are the MEN, MEN, MEN! of the Alcott Cho-rus!" in Gilbert and Sullivan style. I can't imagine what grudge he would have against Wendy. But still, I have to check.

As we warm up, I check his hands, spread under his music folder. No rings. Some people put the pin on a chain, wear it around their neck. Peter's wearing a sweater today, but I don't see a jewelry bulge under the wool.

How else do people wear their pins? I wonder as we sing. Then I remember seeing Taylor's on her bag strap.

As we gather our stuff at the end of class, I check out Peter's backpack. No decoration anywhere.

Peter sees me looking. Smiles. "New sack. You like?"

Shy and embarrassed to be caught, I give a thumbs-up.

And then wonder: When did he switch bags? Why did he switch bags?

Wendy's murder is doing strange things to my head.

Ran into N at the beach. Was wearing my briefest bikini and looking bodacious. Yeah, I think he noticed!

I am reading Wendy's Facebook posts from the summer. If I do go to the police, they'll want to know that Wendy's connection to Nico was more than gossip. And I want to get a sense of what happened between them.

I read:

Here I am, stuck in Amagansett, working in my cousin's restaurant for the summer. How many words for boring are there? Call, text, whatever! Save me!

A few days later: *Check out my new pics from Momo's, a halfway-decent dive where they don't check ID.*

I look at the pictures. Wendy in skirt and bikini top, her arms around some guy at a bar. Not Nico. But in July, I find what I'm looking for.

Ran into a most interesting person at Momo's the other night. Alcott peeps, do the initials NP ring a bell?

According to school scuttlebutt, Nico and Sasha met in the

Hamptons in August. But apparently, in July, he was happy enough with Wendy in Amagansett.

Another insane night at Momo's with N. He's most impressed that I can keep up with him. We discussed the girlfriend sitch. He's dating some snob bitch in the city and has his eye on another one out here. Hilarious.

Ridiculous fun last night. Amazed I'm not in jail! Check out my pics.

I do. Wendy and Nico at a party on the beach at night. Everyone's sitting around a campfire. There's only one picture of the two of them. They're next to each other, but not actually touching. Wendy's holding a marshmallow over the flame, Nico's in his swim trunks holding a beer. She looks pretty, her hair dark in the firelight. They're both laughing.

But things take a bad turn at the end of the month when Nico's girlfriend—Isabel something—comes for a visit.

Saw N with snob bitch gf. Totally acted like he didn't know me. MEN SUCK. PARTICULARLY MARRIED MEN.

Called N on the other night. Got the old What do you want from me line. Why are men never surprising?

No N at Momo's. Man, I'm sick of this scene.

I sit back. So there it is: proof that Wendy and Nico connected at least over the summer. The police will see that, won't they? They'll figure it out.

Maybe, I think. Maybe not.

I feel restless, like I should do something, but I'm not ready to do the one thing I need to. I need to know more. Understand more. Getting my coat, I leave the house and take the subway downtown.

Wendy died in the Sixty-Seventh Street Playground, just off Fifth Avenue. According to the newspaper, her body was found in a circle of greenery planted to give shade and attract butterflies. She didn't get too far into the park, just far enough for someone to grab her and kill her without being seen.

That morning, a jogger taking a rest on a bench noticed a leather bag lying on the ground. Then the body, half pushed under the bushes—as if whoever did it had tried to hide what he'd done, but had run out of time. She saw the back of Wendy's head, but the face was turned away. She saw her shirt and her bra pushed up around her neck. Her arm just lying there in the wet leaves.

It took a moment, the jogger said, to understand that she was looking at a dead girl.

In warm weather, this playground is crazy with kids zooming down the big slide, hopping in the sprinklers or digging quietly in the sand. But on a late afternoon in near winter, it's empty. It rained earlier in the day and the paths are still slick and damp. It's already growing dark. Soon the park lamps will glow to life. But now, the whole world feels gray.

I stare at the spot where Wendy's life ended, trying to feel how it happened. Yellow tape. That's the first thing that tells you, Stay away. It stretches from tree to bush, wrapped around their branches a million times, piss-colored lines crisscrossing this way and that. It looks messy, as if someone didn't care. I hate it, want to rip it all down.

I stand staring at the taped-off area. Wendy lived near here; she and I came here once. It was after school, almost spring. She was smoking a cigarette, legs crossed. Every so often, one of the moms would give her a dirty look for smoking and she'd wag her leg at them. *Yeah, I wear short skirts, too! Total slut, that's right!*

She asked me if I wanted one and I said no. To excuse myself, I said, "It's not like I have much of a singing voice, but . . ."

She frowned, inhaled. "You have a great voice. You're lucky, you have things," she said. Stubbing the cigarette out on the gray stone, she said, "I got squat." She tossed the butt on the cobblestones.

I remember not liking her then, the way she just threw her trash anywhere, felt so sorry for herself. We were already having a lot of bored silences by that time. *Uh, so what do you wanna do? What do you wanna do?* Because we didn't want to do the same things anymore and it was obvious.

I sighed. "What do you want that you don't have?"

"Something that's mine," she said fiercely. "Totally mine that I don't have to share or wait for. Hey, Mom, can we? Not now, honey, gotta work. Hey, Dad, let's . . . Meet my new girlfriend, sweetie. It's like, Take what you get and be happy. Never mind if it's not enough. Never mind if it *sucks*."

She sighed. "Just for once, I want someone to want me more than anybody else. To put me first."

I wanted to ask Wendy why, if that was what she wanted, she always picked guys who were taken. But that would sound like I was blaming her.

Angrily lighting another cigarette, she said, "My mom treats me like I'm this spoiled bitch who demands everything under the sun. And I'm like, Not everything, just what I need, okay?"

This made me uneasy. I did think Wendy asked for too much. You can't have everything you want, I thought. By pushing all the time, you make it so people don't want to give you anything. I wanted to tell her, If I went around demanding things the way you do? Forget it. Someone would slap me back so fast I wouldn't know what hit me.

But I said nothing to Wendy. I was too afraid of hurting her.

Chosen, I think, staring at the yellow tape. You wanted to be chosen, Wendy. That's why you always picked guys who were taken. It wasn't enough to have someone like you, they had to reject someone else. Because that's how it works, right? Someone wins, so someone has to lose. One person's happiness is another person's hurt. That's how you know it's real, when you can look at the girl who didn't get the guy and think, Yeah, he chose *me*.

Someone chose Wendy that night. Someone saw a thin girl with high heels who couldn't run. Maybe she was stumbling a little bit. Maybe she was crying. So lost in her own unhappiness, she wasn't paying attention to anything else.

That's what everyone else thinks.

Here's what I think. Nico and Wendy go to the park. For a gag, they climb the fence. "Hey, let's do it on the slide!" Maybe Nico gets high. Maybe they both do. Wendy gets silly, makes one of her jokes . . .

Or no. Not a joke. Wendy demands that Nico break up with Sasha, be only with her. Nico gets angry . . .

And the next morning a jogger finds a dead girl in the park.

Staring up at the buildings on Fifth Avenue, I wonder, Why didn't anyone hear? Why didn't anyone notice? I turn around, face the playground gate, which they always keep closed. And that's when I see him. A man standing in a navy blue duffle coat, his hands in his pockets. Only, men don't wear duffle coats. Boys do. Beautiful blond boys who look like they attend English boarding schools and ride on the weekends, stealing a nip of brandy from a flask when no one's looking. Boys named Hugh or Rupert who date girls named Sarah and Fenella . . .

But this boy used to live in Queens. With his mom, who's a nurse. His name is Nico Phelps.

He's standing at the gate. Blond hair whipping in the wind.

Staring at the place where Wendy died, as if it's a scene in a movie he's watching.

Why are you here? I wonder. Are you looking for her?

Thinking of her? Remembering?

Remembering what you did?

Nico and I have never spoken since that afternoon on the stairwell. Now for a moment, our eyes meet.

You hurt her, I think. *You hurt people, and this time, you don't get away with it.*

I imagine screaming it out loud, so loud that all those people in all those buildings hear it, so loud that the people walking past this spot stop and remember. So loud that the fact that Nico Phelps killed Wendy Geller can never be not known.

Nico turns, starts walking away. In my head, I'm screaming.

In real life, I utter a small, timid, "Hey . . ."

Nico doesn't hear. No one does.

Walking home, I think about couples and E pins. People do give them to boyfriends or girlfriends they're serious about. But it's not really a cool thing to do. Nice, boring kids do it. Other kids consider it a little . . . tacky.

One thing Sasha's not? Tacky.

But she must have given Nico her pin. It's the only explanation.

Only two people would know for sure. And I certainly can't ask Nico.

Which means I have to ask Sasha.

DAY FIVE

The Alcott School built the Darklis Perry Art Center three years ago. The school added a new floor to the building, a beautiful glass dome with curtains that come down to protect the art from the sun. The equipment is all so fabulous, it makes you yearn to have artistic talent just so you can touch it. State-of-the-art potters' wheels, easels that stand as gracefully poised as dancers, the finest oils, the most delicate brushes, the best drawing pencils. And of course, a huge space dedicated just to sculpture and installation. Generously donated by Sergio Meloni, Sasha's dad.

This might explain why, when after-school time in the studio is a hard-won privilege for most, Sasha can always be found there, working away on her latest creation. It could also be her talent, because Sasha is talented. Or her will. What Sasha wants, she tends to get.

Do I dare do this? I wonder. Confront the gorgeous dragon that is Sasha?

Well, you're going to have to, I tell myself, if you want to help Wendy.

Earlier today, I talked to Lorelei in English class. We chatted about African elephants; saving them is her big passion. It felt ridiculous to be checking out an animal-loving girl in a wheel-chair for murder, but I told myself it was possible Lorelei had lost her ring. But no, there it was, hidden under her blouse on a chain. I couldn't see the whole thing, but from the shape and shadow, it was clearly her E pin.

There's no one in the art studio as I come in. The curtains are half down to keep out the glare. The tables are cleared, the wheels still. All the "wets"—paint, clay, ink—are put away or covered. There's a prayerful feeling, the calm before creation.

And in the back, a scraping sound.

The Sculpture Circle is set off from the rest of the studio, in a private space farthest from the door so you're not disturbed by people coming and going. As I approach, I see various pieces, some covered, some not. Some nearly finished, some just started. Some, I can't tell, to be honest.

Sasha is standing by a vast window, holding a piece of wire in her hands. She grips the ends in her fists, twisting it, pulling it taut. In front of her, a mass of clay, nearly her own height. It's an endless coil—ropes, muscle, wave, I'm not sure—all tangled and fighting. She fixes the edge of the wire to one particularly thick curve and pulls. Strong, hard, determined. Clay peels off, falls to the ground.

I wait till she's done, then say, "Wow."

She knew I was here all along. Stepping back, she says, "Wow good or wow crap?" Her voice is matter-of-fact. She'd rather know if something is crap.

"It's good, Sasha."

She shoots me an amused smile. *Like you would know.* Then she sets the wire aside, wipes her hands with a rag. She's wearing an old black T-shirt and jeans. Her head's wrapped with a piece of cloth, the ponytail high and wild. As she gets ready to work the clay with her fingers, she takes off her rings, drops them into a coffee mug for safekeeping. I watch as they fall in. Some worked silver bands. A pink opal, cloudy and mysterious. The E pin, black and gold.

Say, Sash? How many of those do you have? Two? Don't suppose you'd tell me where you keep the other one. Oh, you gave it to Nico? That's sweet.

Inspecting the piece, she says, "'Sup? I thought you were about vocal arts."

This, I had planned. "A friend of my mom's wants to send her kid here. Art, very big thing for her. I've, uh, been sent to scope."

"Well, it's the best." Sasha takes a drink from a clay-smeared cup, hiding her mouth, lowering her eyes.

There's a pause. I feel I'm losing Sasha to her work. Needing her attention, I blunder, "Wendy liked art."

It's not how I meant to begin. I meant to talk about art and E pins and how many Sasha has and what she's done with them. My mistake gets a chill blast from Sasha, and no wonder. Wendy liking what Sasha likes—I couldn't have gone more wrong.

"She was more into fashion design," I say lamely.

Sasha shrugs. *I couldn't care less what she was into.*

Then, trying to be polite, Sasha asks, "Did you go to the service?"

"Yeah. Did you or Nico—?" I can't quite get the *Nico* out there.

"Me, no. Nico, maybe."

Her voice is casual. If Nico went, if he didn't—she doesn't care either way. Supposedly. But I notice she's really attacking that clay.

"He can be into that," she explains. "Doing the correct thing. His mother's insane about it. It's her reason for being."

A lot of information here. Nico's mine—I know what he's into. I know his mom. We are together. Wendy touched us not at all.

How good a liar are you, Sasha? Do you really not know that Nico left the party right after Wendy? Or do you know, and also know what that might mean—only, you love him, so you're not admitting it to anyone?

Sasha's clever; she's not giving me an easy opening. If I want my answers, I'll have to push—only not so hard that I start a fight. How does Sasha see me? What will she accept from me? She thinks I'm nice, clueless about certain things.

She expects you to be on her side, I realize. Not to go against her. Because no one does.

Wide-eyed and innocent, I say, "I can't believe Nico would go to the Wendy thing."

Sasha looks up. I strain to keep my voice friendly. "I mean, she made things kind of weird for you guys."

Sasha rolls her eyes. "Her crush on Nico? Please. She was just a little louder about it than the rest."

"You and Nico sound serious."

She shrugs. "What's 'serious'?"

I pretend to think. "I don't know. Like, going on vacation serious or giving someone your E pin serious."

Obvious, I think, clumsy, stupid, and obvious.

But all I can do now is put it out there: "I heard that, actually. That you gave Nico one of your E pins."

A flash of something—surprise, anxiety, confusion—across Sasha's face. Quickly replaced by a raised eyebrow. "Yeah, and tomorrow I'm trying out for cheerleading," she says sarcastically. "Give me a break."

In my normal voice, I say, "So, you didn't give him an E pin?"

Sasha narrows her eyes. "Be real. What are you saying?"

The request for *real* hits me; it's something I've always liked about Sasha, she doesn't do fake.

Taking a deep breath, I say, "What happened that night at the party?"

"What happens at every party. Stupidity."

"Sasha . . ."

"*What?*"

"What happened with Nico and Wendy?"

"Nothing."

"That's not what I heard."

"And you care . . . why?"

"Because Wendy was my friend."

No more pretending whose side I'm on. For a moment, Sasha and I stare at each other. I swear, everything I think about Nico, she knows.

Putting her hands on her hips, Sasha says, "Your friend. Let me tell you something about your friend." She gives the word *friend* a twist, making it ugly. "*She* was pathetic. *She* was a liar. *She* had no life, so she tried to steal other people's. And now, even when she's dead, she's still screwing up people's lives." She starts to pace. "Ever since it happened, the cops have been calling my house. My dad told them, Yeah, get a subpoena. Then they show up *here*." Her voice rises. "Yesterday. Do you believe this? That they can do that?"

"What did you do?"

"I was like, Fine, let's get it over with. Yeah, she made noise about my boyfriend. No, nothing happened at the party."

"You know for a fact Nico didn't leave the party?" I say it as quietly as possible.

"He didn't leave." She tosses it off.

". . . for a *fact*, Sasha?"

She hesitates, enough of a person to think about it. "I'm not a wife. I don't monitor every move."

There's a silence as we both absorb what she's just told me. I put my hands in my coat pockets. Sasha goes back to her sculpture. Checking. Smoothing. Perfecting.

I start walking out of the Sculpture Circle.

Behind me I hear: "Just so you know. I've already told the police Nico went home with me that night."

Clattering down the stairs, I head straight for a bathroom. I pull out a handful of paper towel, run it under cold water, and scrub my face with it. I am furious with myself for blowing this conversation—not to mention whatever tiny scrap of a friendship existed between me and Sasha.

She did admit Nico left the party. I got that much. But then she said he went home with her.

No, Rain, she said she told the police he went home with her.

Sighing, I throw the wet paper in the garbage, stare at my reddened face in the mirror.

Sasha, how much do you love this guy? Enough to lie for him? Enough to give him that second E pin?

I go downstairs to the lobby, thinking I'll just go home, sleep on the whole thing, and in the morning, wake up and realize I've been an idiot. Taylor is probably right. Probably on some level, I am angry at all these people. They hurt me, so I want to hurt them back. This might have nothing to do with Wendy whatsoever. . . .

In the lobby, I see Rima sitting on one of the long benches outside the administrative office. Her legs are crossed, her hands flat on the blue silk of her skirt; she looks like an elegant doll. She's humming, but I can't quite make out the tune.

I say, "Hey, Rima."

Breaking off her song, she says, "Rain, hi. God, how are you?"

Surprised by her eagerness, I say, "Good. What are you . . . ?" I gesture around the lobby.

"Oh." Annoyed, she glances at the office door. "Meeting with college advisor. *Avec* parents. Apparently I'm not working up to my potential." She rolls her eyes, then says brightly, "But I've been wanting to talk to you."

Er, you might not say that if you knew I just royally pissed off your best friend, I think. But Rima pats the seat and I sit down.

"I wanted to say I'm sorry I was such a horror the other day." The edge of her dark hair cuts across her cheek as she looks down. "What I said—the whole ding dong thing—not cool."

"I understood."

"I totally thought I was past it, but then when . . ." She shudders, then shakes it off. "Anyway, I'm sorry she's dead and I'm *really* sorry I took my crap out on you."

"I'm really okay with it," I say. And I am. If anyone has a reason to be mad at Wendy, it's Rima.

All of a sudden, I remember Wendy in the hallway. How I told her she was making a mistake going after the top girls; she had to start with their friends, the second-level girls or even third-.

Maybe I should take my own advice.

"I was just talking to Sasha upstairs," I say, praying Rima doesn't ask what we were talking about.

"Working on her piece?" I nod. "She's such an obsessive."

"Yeah," I agree. "Sasha doesn't do halfway."

"No," says Rima. My imagination, or does she sound a little sad?

Tentative, I ask, "Are she . . . ?" I shake my head. "Actually, none of my business."

Rima looks curious. "No—ask."

"Are she and Nico serious?"

"She is, anyway," says Rima. "Unfortunately."

"You don't think he's so great."

"I think he's scum," she says harshly. "A total user."

I feel tingling at the back of my neck. "Why?"

"He's just into her for what he can get. Clothes, connections. The whole status thing. He even—"

She breaks off.

Guessing, I say, "Did he ask for her E pin?"

Rima stares. "How'd you know?"

"I saw him wearing it," I lie.

"Oh, God, Sash'll freak. She made him promise not to wear it at school."

"Why'd she give it to him?"

"He said he wanted it for college interviews. He thinks he's getting into Brown, can you believe that? I told Sasha, any decent college is going to check. But she said if it gave him some extra confidence, why not? She was like, 'It's all ridiculous anyway.'" Rima shakes her head. "She's got this whole Genet beautiful criminal thing going with him. Like somehow because he's not rich, he's more 'real.' I keep telling her he's bad news, but she says I don't understand. Like, yeah, I don't understand when he gets violent and high. I don't understand when he cheats on you. I mean, look at this insanity with Wendy Geller. What she's going through because—"

She breaks off, crossing her arms. "God, sorry, I didn't mean to dump. Sasha says I'm still not over the Seth thing. That I'm 'bitter and suspicious.' Maybe so," she says softly.

This reminds me of what Taylor said to me after Wendy's funeral. "Maybe you just know things Sasha hasn't learned yet."

Rima makes a sad face, then frowns. I look where she's looking, see her parents coming down the hall. Getting up, I say, "Thanks, Rima."

"For what?"

"Being real."

I don't speak. That's what I think as I walk home. It's what people like about me. They can talk—about anything—and I'll just listen, nod, say little things like I understand and Of course. I don't say things like Are you crazy? Or You did a terrible thing. And I never tell anyone else what I've heard.

Never.

But now I have to.

DAY SIX

It all happens much faster than I thought it would. At four o'clock the next day, I am waiting in Mr. Farrell's office to speak with the police. I didn't really want to wait that long—but I wanted to be sure no one was around when I talked to them. I still can't quite believe I'm doing this.

Now I look up at Mr. Farrell, who's standing behind my chair, and ask, "Do you think they'll believe me?"

"Yes." He looks down, squeezes my shoulder.

"Is it weird if I hope they don't?"

"Not at all."

I can't feel my legs. I wiggle my feet to get the feeling back. They tingle, itch—but the sense that I'm about to float away doesn't ease. I can't breathe and my whole body feels buoyant with unreleased air. It is not a nice feeling.

To orient myself, I look at the plain white walls of Mr. Farrell's classroom. At all the empty chairs. At the clock, which says 4:02.

"They're late."

"Only two minutes."

"I don't think I can do this."

"You can," he says. "You can."

If I say No, I can't, again, Mr. Farrell will listen to me. He will let me go. He will let me not do this. But only for today. Tomorrow, the next day, he will find me and he will ask, Have you thought about what you told me?

First thing this morning I told him that they found an E pin near Wendy. That Nico had one. That he left the party close to the same time as Wendy.

His finger curled in front of his mouth, Mr. Farrell admitted, "I knew about the E pin. The police asked us about it."

"So you knew it was someone from school," I said. "When I came to talk to you?"

He nodded. "That's why I felt so strongly that you should talk to the police. I knew you were right, even though I couldn't tell you. The police were anxious to keep the discovery of the pin a secret. They felt there was a real risk Nico would run if he knew they had solid evidence." He hesitated, then added dryly, "And of course, Mr. Dorland was anxious to keep the fact that the murderer went to Alcott a secret for as long as possible."

When he asked if I wanted him to contact the police for me, I said Yes. And Yes again when he asked if I wanted him there when I talked to them.

"What about your mother?" he asked.

I thought of my mom, smiling, reassuring, protective; somehow I didn't want that now.

"I'll be okay," I told him. "I can do this."

And now here we are. And I seriously think I'm going to throw up.

"I think—" But that's as far as I get. The door opens and Detective Vasquez comes in, followed by an actual policeman in uniform. At the sight of the policeman, my stomach twists. I'm breathing, gulping. Mr. Farrell puts both hands on my shoulders.

"It's okay, Rain."

Detective Vasquez sits down, says, "Hello, Rain." I want to ask him to lower his voice when he says my name. Not everyone has gone home, and nobody can hear that I'm doing this. "It's nice to see you again." He glances at Mr. Farrell. "I understand from Mr. Farrell that you have something more you wanted to share with us."

Share. Do I want to share it? I want him to have it. And once I do give it to him, it's his. I never have to think about it again.

"I . . ." I don't know how to start. Why didn't I plan that, what to say? Because somehow I hoped I wouldn't have to.

I look up at Mr. Farrell, who nods.

I mumble, "I don't know what you're thinking these days about who did it. . . ." I check the detective's face for a sign he might say, but it's blank. "I know you talked to Sasha about Nico . . . ?"

"Sasha Meloni," supplies Mr. Farrell. "Nico Phelps." The detective nods.

Twisting my hands, I say, "So—you know . . ." The detective waits. I drop my hands.

"I'm sorry," I say. "I'm doing this really badly."

"You're doing fine, Rain," says Detective Vasquez.

I'm not, I want to tell him. I may talk like an idiot, but I know what sounds right and what doesn't.

Mr. Farrell comes to my rescue. "Detective, you told me about an item you found at the crime scene. Something with an *E*."

"That's right," says the detective.

"At the time, all I could do was confirm that the school gives out E pins and give you a list of the students who have received them. But Rain has learned something that changes the story somewhat."

They're waiting. The pressure to speak gathers on my chest like a weight. I feel like the curtains have parted, the spotlight's hit, and I'm blinking and stupid in the glare.

I'm looking at the floor. Police like it when you look them in the eye. Otherwise they think you're lying. I raise my head.

"You know, right, that Sasha has two E pins?" It's not as bad if they already know it, I think. I'm not really telling them anything. "And you know she's dating Nico?"

"We understand that to be the case."

"Well, sometimes . . ." I duck my head, let my fingers pull at one another. "People who are dating, if they're serious, they give their boyfriend or girlfriend their E pin. Not everybody, but . . ."

On the verge of the first real thing I have to say, I fall silent.

"Take your time," says the detective.

But I don't want to take my time. I want to have this over with. In a rush, I announce, "Sasha gave Nico one of her pins. He wanted it for college interviews. It was about a month ago. Her best friend told me. . . ."

My teeth seize on my tongue. Why? Why did I say that about best friend?

Detective Vasquez gets out his notebook. "What's this best friend's name?"

Panicked, I look at Mr. Farrell. "Do I have to say?"

Mr. Farrell hesitates. "I'm afraid so, Rain."

"Rima Nolan," I say miserably. Now Rima will hate me. Even if she thinks Nico's guilty, she won't want to be the one who gave the police the crucial piece of evidence. Sasha will hate her.

No, I realize, Sasha will hate me. Because I'm the one who went to the police. Rima and Sasha both. My life is about to become a living hell.

Detective Vasquez must sense my panic, because he says, "This is very helpful, Rain. Is there anything else you can tell us?"

"I know Nico left the party to be with Wendy." In my head, I hear Taylor say, "Uh-uh . . ." and change it to "I mean, he left the party right after her. That's why kids told you she left alone."

The detective is checking his notebook. "But you can't tell us if he actually did meet her."

I hesitate. "No, I don't know that."

The detective nods like that's not a problem. "That's fine," he says.

"You believe me, right?"

He looks surprised. "I have no reason not to. I sincerely appreciate your coming forward."

"This was not easy for her," says Mr. Farrell.

"I'm sure it wasn't." Detective Vasquez stands up.

"What happens now?" I ask.

"I'm afraid I can't say just yet. We will certainly be contacting some of the people you mentioned." My stomach tightens. "And we will probably need to contact you again. If you could give us your information one more time."

I do, feeling strangely vulnerable as I write down my name, address, and phone number.

When I'm done, I say, "Can you . . ." I'm about to ask him not to tell people about me. But Rima will know. The second they ask about the E pin.

"I think Ms. Donovan would appreciate if her name could be kept out of it," explains Mr. Farrell. "I'm sure you understand."

The amazing thing about Mr. Farrell, I think, is that he does listen. Even when you don't speak, he hears you.

"Absolutely," says the detective. "And thank you again, Rain."

When he's gone, Mr. Farrell sits down next to me. I feel numb. Even his nearness means nothing. "How are you?" he asks.

"I don't know. I feel . . ."

He reaches out, takes my hand. "What, Rain?"

"I feel like I did something really bad." My voice twists, and I bite my lip as if that will stop the tears.

"Why?" he asks. "Why?"

"I don't know. I just . . . all this stuff is going to happen because of what I said. I wish I hadn't told them anything, I wish they'd just figured it out."

"But they weren't going to," he says gently. "I think they were suspicious of Nico. But they didn't have him at the scene until you told them about the E pin."

This is meant to make me feel better, but it doesn't. Talking to people, finding things out about Nico, reporting them—it all feels weak, somehow.

I remember when I saw him in the park. Just standing there. As if what he'd done could never touch him. He could take life, but nothing could be taken from him. I remember how I wanted to scream at him, to shriek. Shatter his security.

"I wish I'd confronted him," I say, only half aware I'm talking out loud. "Like, I'm terrified he'll find out I talked to the police, but at the same time? I want him to know . . ."

That I did something back, I think. I got him back.

I sit up. This isn't about me, it's about Wendy.

Farrell says, "When things get tough? I want you to remember that you have done a very good thing for your friend."

I look at our hands intertwined.

"Okay."

DAY SEVEN

The next day is Saturday. It is impossible not to remember that last Saturday, I was wondering what would happen at Karina's party. What would Wendy do? How crazy would she be?

My mom has a matinee. I think of staying indoors, then decide, No, out. I don't want to be near the things that will tell me if Nico's been arrested: the phone, the computer, the TV. I want to be away from all of it.

I haven't hung out with Taylor since Wendy's funeral. Dialing quickly, I say, "Hey."

"Oh, hi." She sounds not pissed off. I'm relieved.

"Idea," I say.

"Yes, ma'am."

"Movie? Lunch?"

"Sounds good."

I hesitate. "No Wendy talk?"

She laughs. "Even better."

We pick a serious movie, something political, playing at the art house that's underground near Lincoln Center. As we wait to go in, I think, This is a movie Wendy would never see.

I try to focus on the movie, but it's hard. At one point, I feel my phone buzz. I take my hand off my bag. Try to pretend it didn't happen.

Leaving the theater, we pass a newsstand. I'm afraid to look, but I feel my eyes drawn to the headlines. I have a split second of terror that I'll see my own face, huge and grainy with the word *SNITCH!* over it. But instead, it's just something about the mayor.

I catch Taylor looking at me and say, "I think coffee."

"Definitely coffee," agrees Taylor. We head over to the Bow Wow, which is a coffee bar for dog lovers. There are pictures of all kinds of dogs on the wall. The cups have paw prints on them. The owner's elderly basset hound snoozes behind the counter. It's a little too cute for Taylor, but today, I want to be around life-forms that aren't human.

As we sit down, my phone buzzes again. Steeling myself, I take it out, see the name *Rima Nolan* flashing. I go cold.

It's starting. Right now. They've talked to Rima. It's happening.

"What?" says Taylor.

"Nothing," I say, dropping my phone back in my bag.

We order large coffees. I have a slice of mud cake, try to concentrate as Taylor talks about starting to look for colleges.

"We're juniors," I tell her. "We have eons—don't we?"

She laughs sharply. "Not according to my parents. Not that there's any reason to actually do a search. They just assume I'm going to Columbia, because hey, my brother goes to Columbia, and it has the best journalism school in the country and—" She breaks off moodily.

"And?" I prompt.

"And I kind of want to run off to California and go surfing."

I laugh. "You know? I mean, I love journalism, and Columbia would be awesome, but this is who I've been for, like, my whole life. Maybe I want to try something different. Not just be who I am in high school forever."

"I get you. I do like this you, though."

She grins. "Yeah, well, you're probably stuck with it, so good thing."

My phone buzzes again. This time I don't even look.

Taylor says, "Someone you're avoiding?"

"My mom says it's rude to answer a phone when you're conversing with another person," I say primly.

"Go ahead."

I shake my head. "I don't want to."

Taylor frowns. "Something you want to tell me?"

"Not really," I say.

The phone buzzes two more times while we're at the restaurant. Both times I pretend not to hear it, and both times, Taylor agrees to play along. But as we're leaving, she asks, "How are you with the whole Wendy thing? We didn't talk about that."

"We said no Wendy talk, remember?"

"Yeah, but it's kind of scary they haven't caught the guy, you know?"

There is a question here, but I pretend not to hear it. Instead I give Taylor a hug and say, "I think you'd make an awesome surfer chick."

Walking home, I watch the trees, all shadows now as they wave against the evening sky. I'm on the west side of the park. It's windy out; you can feel the threat in the air.

I'm almost home when my phone buzzes again. Steeling myself, I look, expecting to see Rima's name. But it's not Rima, it's my mom. Vaguely, I remember some promise I made to food shop.

Feeling guilty, I pick up. "Hi, Mom. I'm headed to the market right now. Can I possibly talk you into ginger ice cream?"

There's a pause.

Then, "Honey, forget the food. Just come home."

Something in her voice, a warning. I heard it the day Wendy died. "Why?"

"You didn't hear?"

"No. What?"

"Come home," says my mother, and hangs up.

"In a stunning turn of events, police arrested eighteen-year-old Nico Phelps today in the murder of Wendy Geller. . . ."

I never thought it would be this fast. But there he is on my TV screen. Nico. Wearing a sweatshirt, the hood over his head. Blond hair flying out at the sides, hands cuffed behind his back. There are police all around him, pulling him from the squad car, pushing him into the precinct station. Nico keeps his head down. I can't tell: Is he angry? Frightened?

I did this, I think, feeling sick. This is happening because of me.

"That's the boy," says my mom. "The one whose name I hadn't heard before. You said there was a reason for that."

"Yeah."

"The police are making a big show of this," she says. "They want everyone in the city to know they got him."

Another image. Nico and Wendy on the beach. It must have been taken over the summer.

The TV blares, *"Police initially focused their attention on vagrants known to frequent the park at night. But then, sources tell us, they were* made aware of Mr. Phelps's relationship to the victim, first through her Facebook page, and then through reports from classmates."

Classmates, I think. Plural. Not just me. Other people talked to them.

"These witnesses confirm that the two dated casually over the summer. They also stated that Nico Phelps attended the same party as Wendy Geller on the night of her murder. Video cameras inside the building where the party was held reveal Ms. Geller leaving the party at twelve-fifteen. Nico Phelps can be seen leaving just ten minutes after her, then returning forty-five minutes later."

So Sasha could have been telling the truth. Nico could have gone home with her that night.

After he . . .

"The police report finding scratches on Mr. Phelps's hands and wrists. Tests are being conducted to see if his DNA matches material found under Ms. Geller's fingernails."

Any second now, they'll talk about the E pin. I just pray they don't mention my name.

"Police were further aided in their investigation when they found an item at the scene that indicated that someone connected to the prestigious Alcott School, attended by both Wendy Geller and Nico Phelps, was involved in the killing. Sources say there are some explosive revelations to come. . . ."

If I don't breathe, they won't say my name.

"Nico Phelps has been in trouble with the law before. . . ."

I exhale. My mom clicks the TV off.

"I was watching that," I tell her.

"I can't stand any more." She tosses the remote on the couch.

"But I want to see."

"Why? It's awful, stupid, and ugly."

"Because." I struggle. "I want to hear what they have to say."

"What can they say?"

"I don't know—why he did it?"

"There is no why, darling. Nothing that'll make sense."

"He had to have some reason."

"Yes," says my mother harshly, "the same reason people shake their babies to death. He's a stupid, angry person and she was smaller and weaker than he was. There is no why here."

But there has to be, I think. There has to be a reason I can understand. Otherwise, awful things just happen to people and there's nothing you can do.

I look back at the blank TV, think of that first night when I stared up at my ceiling and imagined a universe where people were just snatched out of life for no reason. I like to think that's not true. That people have . . . weight. Ties. Connections that hold them in this life.

But maybe I've been wrong about that.

That night, I finally get up the nerve to look at my messages. Taylor called. "You were right and I suck. Call me."

Rima called three times. But she only left one message. .

"WHAT DID YOU DO?"

DAY EIGHT

The next day, we drive to my grandmother's house. Normally, I go every other weekend, but today, I'm glad to get out of the city.

In the car, my mom says, "Let's not talk about"—she looks at me—"in front of Grandma. She probably has no idea and I don't think that's so terrible."

"Cool."

But it does feel strange when my grandmother asks how school is and I say, Fine. I'm lying to her and I don't like it.

As we leave, she gives me another photograph. This time of three little girls in old-fashioned, frilly clothing. Pointing to the little one, wide-eyed and seated in front, she says, "Me."

I smile, but my throat catches as I remember seeing Mr. Farrell's picture of his little boy and how I thought of all the pictures Ms. Geller has of Wendy as a baby. Why do babies have to grow up? I wonder stupidly.

On the drive home, my mom says, "I'll be perfectly okay if

you want to skip school tomorrow. I doubt anything productive will happen anyway."

"No," I say. "I'll go."

Even as I wonder, Do people know? Will they be angry? Think I did a great thing?

Please let nobody know, I think to the universe.

DAY NINE

Monday morning. The media swarms the school again. Reporters are everywhere, grabbing kids, offering them microphones, cameras, the chance to be seen, to be heard. To be a part of it.

Some kids run from them. They walk fast, holding their book bags in front of their faces. The reporters chase a little, but not much. Because there are other kids, lots of them, who are willing to talk. Eager, in fact. I look at James Phillips and Darcy Ziegler, both chatting like mad to someone they've never met before. They're smiling, as if they're talking about the happiest thing ever.

No one knows it was you, I tell myself. Which of course is not strictly true because Sasha will remember me asking questions. And Rima knows I was curious about the E pin. From her call, she knows I went to the police. She could put it all together for Sasha, if she wanted to.

I see Karina next to a slick guy with too much hair. He's holding the mike out to her as if it were a lollipop.

Angry, she says, "Personally, I just can't believe this is happening. Nico's a good guy. People shouldn't decide things before they know all the facts."

Karina also knows I suspected Nico. She is someone to stay

138

away from. Turning to circle around her, I hear, "Hi, just looking for some reaction to the arrest of Nico Phelps. Were you friends with Nico or Wendy?"

I look around, expecting to see a person. Instead what I see is a massive eye, pitch-black and trained on me. A microphone hovers in front of my face. My stomach lurches. I feel near tears.

"Any comment?"

I race into the building. Inside, everyone's in tight little groups; safety in numbers. Also, information. Everyone talking about what they heard, what they saw, what they think. Ms. Laredo wanders around trying to get people to class. "Let's move along, people. Let's all just . . ." No one listens.

By my locker, I hear Daisy Loring say, "This is not a surprise. The guy's a criminal. I don't know why they didn't lock him up before."

Ernie Wolfert, who is a friend of Nico's, says, "You don't know what happened. You weren't there." He stalks down the hall.

And that is not the only argument I hear. People swap stories of this awful thing Nico did or weird thing he said. But often, there is someone to defend him—or to point out that Wendy "pushed him pretty hard," or "we don't know what Wendy did to make him lose it."

I duck into the nearest bathroom. Throwing water on my face, I remember how I thought it would be better once everyone knew the truth.

A toilet flushes, and I jump. I wait for the door to open, but it stays closed.

I call, "Hey there. You okay?"

No answer. I tap on the door and it swings open. Inside is Jenny Zalgat.

"I'm hiding," she says, "as you can probably tell."

"Too insane?"

"Totally. I still don't get it. I mean, what? They snuck out of the party and he killed her in the park? Why?"

"That's what I keep wondering," I say.

"You don't think she was pregnant, do you? It always seems like someone gets pregnant in these things. Like on TV."

"Not TV."

"Yeah, unfortunately." She pulls at the toilet paper, letting it slide onto the floor. "I mean, did you think he could do it?" She takes my silence as a no. "Not that I was a huge fan. Nico always treated me like I was some brain-dead nobody. I never said it to Wendy, though, and I feel awful about it. Like I was this big cheerleader for her. 'Yay, get Nico, yay!' I wish I'd said what I really thought."

"Me too." I try to think of something good that might come out of this horror. "Anyway, it'll make people feel better to know they caught the guy. Wendy's family." Remembering the family, I think of the funeral. Ellis, pretending he and Wendy were still together. Now he'll have to face the fact that Wendy really did sneak out with Nico.

"Not so fun for Ellis," I say.

Jenny makes the tiniest face. "Yeah, no doubt."

Feeling the tug of something hidden, I say, "He was really into Wendy. I thought they were nice together."

"Yeah. Unfortunately, Wendy told me there was zero spark." Jenny's voice is harsh, and I must look surprised, because she says, "Sorry, I don't mean to be mean. But he's such a drama-holic. I can't stand how he's been pretending they were all in love when she died. Of course he knew it was over."

"Right," I say, keeping it neutral.

Jenny's talking fast now, maybe babbling through the stress. "You know, the week of the party, he was like, 'Oh, are you going to Karina's party Saturday? And do you want to go together?' Wendy said, 'Um, not such a great idea.' She tried to be nice about it, 'cause she knew he still liked her. But I guess the great Ellis felt she was pitying him, 'cause he got really pissed off."

I think. "I don't remember him at the party."

"Yeah, he didn't even come after all that. Guess he didn't want to see the truth slapping him in the face."

Then where was Ellis that night? I wonder. But before anything comes clear, the bell rings. Time for first period.

Jenny goes to a sink, throws water on her face. "I'm thinking of asking my parents for a transfer."

I say, "Oh, anyplace else would be so boring."

"Perfect."

We leave the bathroom, step out into the hallway. And then it happens. I am smashed. Full-force, right up against my side—arm, shoulder, head. I fall so fast I'm barely aware of falling. Until I hit the floor.

Struggling up on one elbow, I see Sasha, standing over me. She's holding her bag by the strap. Instinctively, I raise my arm in front of my face, feeling the pain of the blow before the bag clobbers the top of my head.

"Bitch!" More blows—the buckles on the bag strike my face, the hard points of her boots slam into my back. Helpless, I kick back, feet flailing, not to hurt, just to get her away from me. As I do, I'm aware of other people, standing, watching.

Rima, I think, Rima must have told her we talked.

"Stupid! Blabbermouth! Gossiping! Bitch!" Every word,

another hit or kick. "Sticking up for your whore friend, right? Bzz, bzz, bzz, oh, she said this and he did that. Ooh, let's tell the police, let's feel all important. You don't know *anything! Anything!* This is people's lives!"

On *lives*, the bag swings into my face. Not a hard hit—Sasha's so angry now her aim is off. Still, I curl up into the smallest thing possible. My eyes are pressed into my knees, my fingers grip the back of my head. Agony as Sasha stomps on my hair, shrieking, "What gives you the right? To screw with people's lives? What gives you the right?"

Then I hear, "Okay, enough." Sasha must lunge for me again, because again it's said, *"Enough."*

Mr. Farrell. He tells everyone, "Clear out, now," tells Sasha she needs to go home, he will make sure it's okay.

Meanwhile, I hope to sink through the floor, through the carpet and wood, into some netherworld where no one can see me ever again.

What gives you the right? To screw with people's lives? What gives you the right?

Wet on my face. Blood? I taste. No. Just tears and snot. I didn't even know I was crying. My hair is loose, it hangs over my face like a raggedy curtain. I see one chopstick under the water fountain. The other, snapped in two.

"Rain?"

"Go away."

"I'm not going away."

A hand on my arm. "Please, I really just need to be by myself."

"Well, you can't be." There's something amused in his voice; this is not so serious. It gives me the courage to look up. He's smiling.

"Not in the middle of the hall," he says. "Come on. Up you get."

He holds out his hand. I take it. Am lifted up.

Half an hour later, I think how strange it is that one of my biggest fantasies has come true. I am sitting alone with Mr. Farrell. Not in school, but in a restaurant. That he took me to. And I could not care less.

I ache all over. My scalp. My legs. My arms. But nothing hurts as much as understanding that Sasha could have done anything she wanted to me and there was nothing I could do to make her stop.

I've felt helpless before. But to have no power? When someone is destroying you and it's for real, not names? I didn't know what that was before.

A bowl of lentil soup slides in front of me. Then a chocolate-frosted donut. I don't remember the last half hour. Did I order this? I look up.

Embarrassed, Mr. Farrell says, "I didn't know what you'd want. You seem like a lentil soup kind of girl."

"I love lentil soup."

He smiles, relieved. "But, uh, donuts always make me feel better. So." He busies himself with his own soup. Which is chicken noodle.

All those people watching. *Oh, man, Rain's getting stomped. Let's do nothing.* Do they all hate me, think I deserved to get stomped?

Isn't anyone on Wendy's side? Pointing out that, hey, Nico killed someone. He should be punished for that. But maybe some people don't think so. Maybe it's still, Come on, it's just Nico. So he killed someone. It's not like she was cool or anything.

I look at Mr. Farrell. "You don't have to do this."

"Do what?"

"Take care of me. You must have classes."

"Ms. Petrie's subbing." He dips his spoon into the soup. "And of course I have to take care of you, Rain. You were attacked. Do you want to talk about it?"

"What's to talk about?"

"How you feel, maybe?"

"How I feel is it doesn't matter how I feel."

"Please don't say that, of course it matters. You did the right thing, speaking up."

Speak up. My whole life, people have been telling me to speak up—and what happens? I end up on the floor with someone's foot in my face.

I look around the diner. It's not the one Taylor and I go to, but it's familiar. I've been here before. . . .

"I got dumped in this diner," I tell Mr. Farrell, remembering.

"Oh, dear," says Mr. Farrell. "Bad choice on my part."

"Not your fault. It only lasted, like, a month." I draw my feet up on the seat, lean against the wall. "The guy didn't even have the guts to look at me. He was texting the whole time. Even when he said, 'You know, it's, like, not working out.'"

"I'm sure I don't have to tell you boys this age are . . . flawed."

"Oh, girls this age are wonderful," I say sarcastically.

"They're better." He raises his hands in comic self-defense. "I can say this. I'm a man. God, I remember myself . . ." He turns to a painting on the wall as if it's a mirror that shows him his younger self. "Stupid doesn't even begin to cover it."

I smile. "Don't tell me you dumped nice girls too."

"Never got the chance." He grins. "I ignored all the nice

girls who might have liked me. I'm pretty sure there weren't that many," he adds quickly.

"I'm sure there were a few," I say.

"I didn't notice. I only had eyes for the ones I couldn't get." He picks up his coffee. "Don't waste too much energy on high school boys, Rain. A man would have to be forty-five to match your maturity."

Thirty-five would do just fine. I am so close to saying it, to put it all right out there and see what he does with it.

Go for it, tigress.

But I don't. Not for any moral reason. One of the things Mr. Farrell—likes, is into, whatever words you want to use—about me, is he thinks we're the same. Dreamers. Not doers. Thinkers. Not talkers. Selfishly, I want to keep him thinking just that.

"I don't know if I can go back to school," I tell him.

"No, certainly not," he says, gesturing for the check. "Come on, I'll walk you home."

It's a funny weather day. Heavy clouds, but here and there, patches of blue sky edged with sunlight. As we walk uptown, the school neighborhood gives way to my home turf, which is a little funkier in ways both good and bad. I point out the deli where you get amazing olives; Mr. Farrell nods to the bookstore run by the crazy guy. I say I love that place too. I tell him about the old movie theater that went out of business, its big empty marquee still up.

A little farther is Columbia University, which feels like a medieval town to me, with its old buildings and big open squares. I have a drifty fantasy that someday I will go to school there. Mr. Farrell will go too, do some kind of graduate thing. A little apartment, eating Chinese takeout on the floor . . .

I know I should say I'm fine, he doesn't have to do this. I know I should let him get back to school.

I ask, "Won't Dorland be upset that you're cutting?"

"I'm the acting head of the upper school," he says dryly. "I'll just tell him you were thinking of suing the school and I had to talk you out of it."

Joining in the joke, I ask, "Should I sue? Maybe I'll sue Sasha—she has more money than Alcott."

"If you need a witness—"

"I'll cut you in."

"Thank you."

He likes it when I say the wrong thing, I realize. It's okay.

I ask, "What would you do? With a million billion dollars?"

He puts his hands in his pockets. "Quit my job. Finish my book. Move to the country."

"What's your book about?"

"Oh"—he sighs—"unhappy young man in love with a girl he can't have."

"Maybe he just needs to speak up." I must be feeling better if I can joke about speaking up.

I look to see Mr. Farrell's reaction and notice we're in front of a newsstand. Wendy's face, everywhere you look. But one cover stands out, the *Herald,* the paper that reporter Stella writes for. They don't have the smiling picture from the yearbook. It's an image from the Facebook video, the one where Wendy says to Nico, *I am going to get you.* She's grinning, leaning forward. They've cropped the photo so your eyes are drawn to look down her shirt.

Screaming words: DEATH IN THE PARK! ROMANTIC TRYST TURNS DEADLY!

Then in smaller letters, EXCLUSIVE: EXPLOSIVE NEW EVIDENCE THAT LINKS CLASSMATE NICO PHELPS TO THE CRIME!

The E pin. I reach for one of the newspapers. Mr. Farrell says, "God, please—leave it. It's obscene."

I mumble, "I know, it is." But I can't help myself. I take one of the papers, throw the guy a dollar. To Mr. Farrell, I say, "I just want to make sure I'm not being written about."

He's so horrified, I feel I can't look now. Folding the paper, I put it in my bag. "I can't believe what they're doing to her."

"She's dead. She has no power," he says in a numb voice. "They can do anything."

As we walk, I think about how unfair it is that people can say anything about Wendy.

Then Mr. Farrell stops, says, "I believe this is your block."

It is. "You know where I live?"

"At Alcott, you have to memorize the addresses of every student," he says, deadpan.

"Come on."

He smiles down at the ground, shrugs in his coat. "I looked it up. After that first time we talked. I remembered it because I happen to live ten blocks up that way." He nods uptown.

Then he says, "Also, I wrote you a letter."

"But you didn't send it?"

He shakes his head.

"Not fair."

"It was nothing important. Just . . . about Wendy."

A letter. He wrote me a letter. That means he thought about me when I wasn't there. He thinks about me, wants to tell me things.

Then he switches the subject. "I'll inform Mr. Dorland of

what happened. I imagine we'll arrange some kind of leave for Sasha. She's going through a terrible time."

This is good news, but I barely care. I'm about to remind him of that letter when I hear, "What on earth are you doing here?"

My mother's voice. It is a famous voice; many people know it. I know it best of all.

"God, Mom . . ."

She is standing in what she calls her purple poof, a down coat that covers her from neck to foot. She is carrying her black leather bag, filled with opera scores.

Now she is smiling—but not—at Mr. Farrell. Her eyes are a warning. *Explanation necessary.*

"Mom, this is Mr. Farrell. He teaches at my school."

"Have we met?" Mom is doing sweet and confused, but she knows the answer.

"No, we haven't," says Mr. Farrell, offering his hand. "I don't have Rain in a class, but there was an incident at school today and—"

"He stopped Sasha Meloni from kicking the crap out of me," I say cheerfully, knowing my mom can have no argument with Mr. Farrell now.

"What?" Immediately, my mom starts patting, squeezing me here and there. "Have you seen a doctor?"

"The school checked me out, Mom."

"Meaning they took your temperature and gave you an aspirin." She starts fishing in her bag. She's going for the cell phone.

"Mom, I'm *fine*."

"She really does seem fine, Ms. Donovan," Mr. Farrell says. My mom shoots him a look and he finishes weakly, "I just wanted to make sure she got safely home."

There is a pause. The phone slides quietly back into the bag. "All right," says my mother. She still wants to yell, I can feel it. Instead she says, "Well, thank you, Mr. Farrell. I'm sorry I was . . . I overreacted."

"Not at all."

"Let's go home," she says to me. Voice bright, arm around me, means love. But also: no argument.

"Good-bye, Mr. Farrell," she says.

Me, I just look back. See him watching me go. He's looking at me, I think. He sees me.

"Rough day."

My mom is making a pot of tea. A plate of cookies is on the table. I want to tell her I'm full up on lentil soup and donuts. But this is something she needs to give me, and if I don't take it, there will be questions.

Now she asks, "Tell me what happened with Sasha."

I reach for a cookie. "I don't know if you know, but she and that guy Nico were dating." My mom turns, shocked. "So—she's a little freaked right now."

"I can imagine. But why take it out on you?"

I turn the cookie plate with one finger, avoiding my mom's eyes. I don't know how to tell her I talked to the police without her. That somehow it was something I had to do on my own. And she would freak if she knew I had talked to Stella the reporter.

"Well, I have been thinking that maybe Nico might have done it."

"You didn't tell the detective that," she says, surprised.

"I wasn't sure then. And it seemed like they weren't interested in Nico. But I talked to Sasha about what happened that night and"—I shrug—"I guess I made it a little obvious that I thought he was guilty."

"I'm calling her parents."

"No, Mom, don't," I beg. "Mr. Farrell said they're going to suspend Sasha. I won't have to deal with her."

I can feel my mom watching me. She knows there's something missing. The kettle whistles and she turns back to the stove. Pouring water into the teapot, she says casually, "Tell me about Mr. Farrell."

Wary, I say, "He's a teacher. A nice guy."

My mom wraps a towel around the pot while the tea steeps. She comes to the table, sits down. "He likes you."

I say, "He was being kind. It was a hideous day."

"Okay. He was being kind. And he likes you. And you . . . ?" I'm silent. "You like him, too."

"In that . . . totally harmless teacher crush way." I start rolling a napkin with my fingers, see how tight I can get it.

"Don't be around him."

I look up, expecting my mom to be smiling. She's not. "Mom—"

"I'm very serious about this. He's married, I saw the ring."

"Yeah, with a little kid. Who he happens to adore, so I don't think . . ."

She shakes her head. "The one has nothing to do with the other. Nothing. A man can be married and . . ."

And then she has to stop. Because, of course, my dad was married when she fell in love with him. Still is. And had kids he probably adores. And one he doesn't know—me.

"Nothing's going on, I promise." My mom isn't satisfied, I can feel that. "I wouldn't do that, Mom, come on."

But I shock myself by realizing I've just told my mother a lie.

I didn't mean to. But what I said is not true. I would absolutely do it if Mr. Farrell gave me a chance.

Then I think, No, no, no. Wait a minute. This is not me. Fun to think about? Yes. Fantasize, dream over, absolutely. But it would never happen because . . .

Because you don't have the guts, says a voice.

"This is a hard time," I hear my mom say. "But honey, please. Don't play with this."

"I'm not playing." I say it fiercely, unsure whether it means that I'm not doing anything with Mr. Farrell or that my feelings are real.

My mom says, "Is this about your . . . ?" Then goes silent.

Because she was about to say my dad. And that's something we never talk about.

The silence is awful, everything we're not saying jagged and spiky between us. Wanting a way out, I take the newspaper out of my bag. Opening it, I find the headline, EXCLUSIVE! EVIDENCE PUTS NICO AT THE SCENE OF THE CRIME!

Stella, just as I thought.

An inside source told this newspaper that police found a piece of jewelry stamped with an E at the crime scene. Our investigation has further learned that the prestigious Alcott School gives out what are called E pins to outstanding students. While not an outstanding student himself, Nico Phelps is said to be dating E pin recipient Sasha Meloni, the daughter of . . .

"Oh, God, don't read that trash," says my mother.

I feel a flare of anger. Don't talk to this person, don't watch that, don't read this, don't know anything. If my mother had her way, my life would be one closed box, with me locked inside.

My cell rings and we both jump. "Probably Taylor." I slide off the chair, glad of the chance to end the conversation.

On the way to my room, I check who it is.

Stella Walcott.

Two thoughts flash in my brain: No way am I answering this, and Something's happened, I have to know what.

Clicking, I answer, "Hello?"

"Hello, Diner Girl. Or—should we make it Rain?"

Hearing Stella say my name is strange, but I think I prefer it to Diner Girl. "We should."

"I was just wondering if you had any reaction to the arrest."

Whatever I say to Stella, I say to the world, so I have to be careful. "If he did it, I hope they find him guilty."

"I hear the girlfriend attacked you. True?"

"It was no big thing."

"She thinks he's innocent, I gather."

"Guess so."

"You read my article?"

"Um-hm."

"I didn't mention you, right? You can trust me, you know."

Remembering that awful, leering picture of Wendy, I decide to let that one sit.

"How's Nico?" I ask.

"Lawyered up. Not talking. Except to say, Never saw her, never touched her, didn't do it."

"Does he know about the E?" I want to know if Nico knows I'm involved.

"The police told him they found one at the scene. At first he said he didn't have one, but they told him they knew the girl-friend gave him one."

I hold my breath, somehow expecting her to say, "And they told Nico YOU told them that, Rain!" But she doesn't.

"What'd he say to that?"

She snorts. "He claims he lost it."

I hesitate. "Do you think they'll find him guilty?"

She pauses. "I think the defense is going to work real hard to make the victim seem guiltier."

"Maybe you could not help them with that."

"Maybe. Look, I have to go. Do me a favor? Don't spread it around that I told you about the little silver thing. This is a big story for me, and I don't want my source knowing I share info with teenagers."

I must be tired. Nothing computes. "What little silver thing?"

"The—" Stella lowers her voice "You know. The E."

I think of the ring on Sasha's finger, that flash of black and gold. I wait for Stella to say, *Oh, wait, sorry, gold.* Because it has to be gold. Black and gold are the school colors. That's why the E pins are black and gold.

Dread takes hold of me like cold hands: maybe what they found wasn't an E pin.

"What does the E look like?" I ask, trying to sound casual. "I mean, is it an earring, a—"

I hear a phone ring. Stella says, "Hold on, Rain. . . ."

A click. A moment later, she's back. "I gotta go, kiddo. Hey, listen. Be happy—they got the guy who hurt Wendy." The line goes dead.

But, I think. But. But. But . . .

Maybe they didn't get the guy.

Frantic, I assemble all the evidence against Nico: Wendy's obsession, the scratches, the surveillance camera. He left after she did. He's a liar. He hurts people.

And I am not the only one who thinks he killed her, I think wildly. Mr. Farrell thinks so. Rima thinks he's evil. Jenny doesn't like him.

But not liking him is not the same as thinking he's a murderer, I remind myself. And until the DNA tests come back, the only thing that links Nico to the crime is the E pin.

That you told the police was his.

But if what they found at the scene was silver, then it can't be the E pin Sasha gave to Nico.

Which means I lied to the police. The realization knocks the breath out of me. Whether or not I meant to, I put an untrue thing out in the world. Other people do it all the time—*She's retarded. He sells his mom's Xanax. She fools around with her brother. His parents paid to get him into the school.* I've always hated that, the ugly things we say and think about each other not caring if they're true or not.

I *did* care, I think desperately. It wasn't that I didn't care. I did all this because I cared about Wendy.

Only, that doesn't make it right.

DAY TEN

"Mr. Farrell?"

He looks up from the library table. "Rain. It's very early. . . ."

I fiddle with my bag strap. "I know you're working on your book, but could we talk? I was going to call you last night, but it was late, and I didn't want to . . . It is actually important, I promise."

Immediately, he starts gathering his things. "Of course. Let's go to my room."

As we walk into his classroom, Mr. Farrell closes the door and says, "You should know that the school decided that Sasha would take a two-week leave of absence."

I wince.

Mr. Farrell misunderstands, saying, "I'm sure after two weeks, enough will have come out about the case that she'll realize that . . ." He trails off. ". . . she made a mistake."

"She didn't," I say, sitting down.

"How do you mean?" He sits too.

"Sasha didn't make a mistake. She was absolutely right to be furious with me. Mr. Farrell—what I told the police? It wasn't true. I thought it was, but . . ." I dig my fingers into the table edge. "I've done something really wrong and I have to make it right."

"Rain, slow down. Start at the beginning."

"So, this reporter? Who told me about the E pin?" He nods. "Last night she called me again, wanting more dirt on the case. I didn't give her any, but just before she hung up, she said the E pin was silver."

Mr. Farrell just looks puzzled. I explain, "They're not silver, they're gold. Black and gold, right?"

He nods slowly. "The school colors."

"If it's silver, it's not Sasha's E pin. Which means the police don't have anything to tie Nico to the scene of the crime. Which is kind of a big deal, right? I have to tell them."

Now Mr. Farrell will tell me what an idiot I am, that we have to go to the police right now and I'll be lucky if they don't charge me.

But instead, he sits back, says, "Let's think." He sighs as he does so. Then says, "Well, for one thing, this woman is a tabloid writer."

"So?"

"How reliable is she? Can you really trust her to remember a detail like gold or silver?"

For a moment, I'm stumped. I had expected Mr. Farrell to agree right away.

I say, "She's the one who told me about the E pin to begin with. She obviously knows things."

"But if what you're saying is true, then it's not even an E pin. Why would you trust the person who gave you the wrong information?"

"Because . . ." I struggle. Then think of something. "Did the police show you what they found?"

He shakes his head. "They described it, asked if we had any idea what it might be. I said I couldn't possibly be certain, but the school did give out pins with E's on them for achievement. We gave them a list of current students who had received one. We did ask them not to mention the pin unless it was absolutely necessary. We didn't want to start a rumor flood."

"But they must have seen it," I say. "Talking to people. They have to know—"

Then I remember Sasha dropping her rings into the cup. The little bump under Lorelei's shirt. The clean strap of Peter's bag. Taylor telling me she didn't have her bag when she talked to the police. All those people I talked to, I didn't see the pin once. The police would have had to ask to see it. Which Mr. Dorland basically asked them not to do.

"You should know: Nico is out on bail," says Mr. Farrell abruptly. "As of late last night."

Nico free—possibly knowing I accused him. I fight the feeling of panic.

"Do you really think Nico Phelps is innocent?" Mr. Farrell asks gently.

Nico standing at the playground, no expression on his face. His finger in my mouth, twisting, hurting.

"No. But I still need to tell the police. I have to make my part of it right."

"Rain, your part of it is right already." Mr. Farrell leans forward. "It's understandable that you're having doubts, especially after what happened yesterday with Sasha. But Nico has lawyers, very good ones. If there's a flaw in the case, they'll catch it. Do me a favor. Think about this. The trial isn't happening to-morrow."

But it's happening every day in the papers, I think. This morning on my way to school I saw a headline: CLASSROOM KILLER. HOW NICO PHELPS WENT FROM MONEY TO MURDER.

Also: IT'S A MATCH! SKIN FOUND UNDER WENDY GELLER'S FINGER-NAILS MATCHES NICO PHELPS'S DNA!

Which means he probably did kill her, I think, feeling suddenly exhausted. Mr. Farrell is right: I don't know what I know anymore.

"Just sit and think," says Mr. Farrell. "Is there anyone else who could have murdered Wendy? Really think. And if you can think of someone and you want to go to the police, I will go with you."

From his expression, I can tell, Mr. Farrell doesn't believe I'll come up with anyone else who could possibly have killed Wendy.

Now is probably not the time to tell him I already have come up with someone. Because the thought of it makes me ill.

Last night, after I hung up with Stella, I thought long and hard. If they didn't find a school pin, what does the *E* they did find stand for? Probably a name—but whose?

I thought of Nico's name in the yearbook. Nicholas Andrew Phelps. Not a single *E* anywhere. So, who of Wendy's friends had an *E* initial?

When it came to me, I wondered why I hadn't thought of it before. It seemed so obvious. But I didn't see it because I didn't want to. I was too hung up on Nico.

I opened Wendy's Facebook page. Searching for the *E*'s in

her life, I found Elodie, a friend from Long Island, who weighs maybe ninety pounds, and a cousin Etan, who lives in California.

And Ellis, of course. Everybody's guy. Who's been just a little off since this happened.

Yes, Rain, maybe because a girl he loved was murdered.

Or maybe something else.

Ellis and Wendy started dating in September. But when I opened Wendy's page, I saw that they were flirting at the end of last year. In May, Ellis posted *Ellis likes this* about one of Wendy's pictures. In June, Wendy complained about having to work in Amagansett and he answered, "Aw, poor Wens! Try the summer with your mom and aunties in Ahmedabad." They back-and-forth about the ending of a movie, "Awesome!" "Sucked!" and compete to see who loves *True Blood* more.

Then in September, Wendy wrote:

Everybody sit down or you may faint from shock. I have a boyfriend! No, really. And he's an official Nice Guy. (I know, what's he doing with me, right?) Check him out.

Pictures of Wendy and Ellis snuggling in the rec room—or wreck room, ha ha—at school. In Bendel's, wearing silly hats. A nice one of Ellis sitting at Wendy's kitchen counter.

The friends approved, chorusing, Love this! OMG—you're doing single guys now? I gotta sit down. Jealous! Hate you, bitch. Nah, just kidding . . .

For a few weeks, it's all Ellis. He's her "sweetie," "the best." They do everything together. Wendy moans about her mom complaining about the text bills.

Then,

Feeling low. Turns out nice guys are not for me. Hope I wasn't a bitch about it.

One friend writes, "I'm sure you were!" Another, "Knew it! I win the poll!" But mostly, it's "Oh, no!s" and "Big hugs!"

Then a week later,

Advice, please, bitchettes. I'm not into do-overs. But recently, I saw someone I "knew" a few months back—I'll call him The Hot One. There was a definite connection, but he said the little woman wouldn't under-stand, blah, blah. I was kind of pissed, as you may remember. Today he gave me that look. Should I? He is sex on a stick. Of course, there is a wifey.

The Hot One is Nico. Wifey must be Sasha. So Wendy's flirtation with Nico probably started before she dumped Ellis. But she didn't want to say so in case Ellis was still reading.

Things moved pretty fast from there.

Met up with The Hot One outside school. I have the feeling he's tired of what he's getting at home.

Five-star day! Saw The Hot One.

No-star day. Hot One sticking with wifey. Didn't stop him getting some in the park.

I thought, If I am Ellis reading this, I am not having fun.

Her friends weighed in. "Been there, done that. Move on, babe." "Dump the loser." "Hey, here's a wild idea! Try someone without a girlfriend."

Wendy wrote back, *Yeah, can't do that. This is kind of real.*

Then a week later, Wendy posted COMMITMENT! with a link to a video. I clicked on the link, saw Wendy in Jenny's room. They're rolling around on the floor, holding the phone up, laughing hysterically.

Wendy gasps, "Okay, I'm making it official. I want Nico Phelps! Nico, you hear? I want you!"

"Girlfriend alert," giggles Jenny.

Wendy fake frowns. "Oh, yeah, gee. Oh, wait, I don't give a crap. Sorry, Sashy. Nico's mine. And I don't mean in that bathroom quickie way, I mean for real. Because you don't get him, and I do. So he should be mine. Step aside, girlfriend."

It occurred to me: I hate this voice, her Wild Wendy persona. It's sort of her—but more what everyone decided she was. It's like she's playing a part on some gross reality show. How did that happen, Wendy? I wondered. Why did you let them make you into that?

I looked to see if Ellis responded to any of this, but he was silent.

After that, it's all little updates on Nico. *Saw N in hallway. N talked to me in cafeteria. Caught N checking out my, er, fine new top.*

It's not enough for the friends. They tease her. *We want action! You're losing your touch, girlfriend. Promises, promises. Turn up the heat!*

And then the video made two days before she died, the one that is now Wendy to most of the world: "This is a message from Wendy Geller to Nico Phelps. Nico, you best be listening. Because two days from now at Karina Burroughs's party, I am going to get you. I am going to get you and you are going to love every moment."

Leaving Mr. Farrell's classroom, I wonder, Could what I'm thinking about Ellis be true? In a flash, I remember what Jenny said: "I guess the great Ellis felt she was pitying him, 'cause he got really pissed off."

Pity. I think of how Ellis's black hair is always just so. His black-and-white-checked sneakers, his styling geek cardigans. The way he always makes a joke if people are paying attention to someone other than him.

He wouldn't be into pity. At all.

And I have history class with him this afternoon.

If you ever read the Alcott brochure, you will learn that one of the things that distinguishes Alcott is its belief in "experiential learning" and "exploration of the rich cultural environs of the city."

Which, loosely translated, means "field trip." Art class, you go to MoMA. History, the Metropolitan. Science, the natural history museum and the Rose Center (where a few kids always manage to sneak off to the space show and get high).

So, today in social studies, we're going to Central Park. To study public space and what it means to a community.

Some of the parents complained, saying this was a bad idea. But our teacher, Ms. Wilentz, told them we wouldn't be anywhere near the area affected by "recent tragic events." She's not one to change her mind.

In the park, Taylor and I walk toward the back of the group as Ms. Wilentz talks about how Frederick Law Olmsted saw the park as a place where everyone who lived in the city could gather, rich and poor. Not too many people are gathered today; it's a gray, chilly afternoon. We see a few brave joggers, determined dog walkers with batches of four-legged clients, the occasional park worker in green, tiredly picking up trash.

I tell myself I should be listening to Ms. Wilentz, who's an amazing teacher. Or thinking about Frederick Law Olmsted.

But I'm watching Ellis. He's walking toward the front of the group, Lindsey right beside him. I'd love to catch up with him, ease into a conversation. (*Say, Ellis, why did you act like you and Wendy were still together at the funeral? Were you so upset because Wendy was dead? Or because you killed her?*) But that won't be possible with Lindsey around. She's superprotective.

Ms. Wilentz says, "Okay, everyone, let's split into teams and get to work."

The assignment is to walk around the park and see how Olmsted's vision is holding up. We have to grade things that we see as belonging to everyone, that belong to most people, and that belong to a few. Like Sheep Meadow—open, free, belongs to anyone. The carousel which costs money, but not that much, belongs to most people. Well, that's what I say. Taylor, my partner, says no one on a budget would pay for a stupid merry-go-round ride, so it belongs to a few.

"You don't know what people will and won't pay for," I say, watching Ellis out of the corner of my eye.

"It's reasonable to draw conclusions based on economic circumstance," she says sweetly, knowing she'll win the argument, that we'll put "a few" and get an A.

"Fine," I say absently, wondering, *Ellis—how could you be so clueless about Wendy's Nico obsession?*

Taylor is waving her hand in my face. "Hello? Bathrooms? All or most?"

I see Ellis walking toward the bathrooms, for once free of Lindsey.

"Well, right now, bathrooms are for me," I say, handing Taylor my clipboard. "Be right back."

As I walk toward the bathrooms, I realize I have no idea how to start this conversation. Nico's arrest. I'll begin with that, see where it goes.

I'm trying to decide if I should say "Hey, Ellis—wait up!" or just plain "Ellis!" when he turns suddenly and smiles.

"Rain—" he says, and gives me a huge hug.

I've been so wrapped up in my vision of Ellis the twisted killer, I'm thrown. Especially when he says, "I heard about Sasha attacking you. That's crazy."

"Uh, yeah," I stammer. "Well, guess it wasn't the best day for her."

"No." He nods sympathetically. "But still. Not your fault she was dating a murderer."

I scan his face, his voice. No hint of uncertainty. If Ellis doesn't absolutely believe Nico's the killer, he's doing an amazing job of hiding it.

I say, "Yeah, but I kind of let Sasha know I thought Nico killed Wendy."

"So?"

I look at the ground. "I let the police know it too. Please don't spread that around."

"Okay. But I think it's great." He looks away. "I wish I'd ratted him out. But I didn't know—" He shrugs.

"You didn't think he did it?"

"No." He looks at me. "I know I'm probably the only person in the world who thinks this. But in my gut, I never thought Wendy'd go through with the whole . . . Nico thing." His voice sours with disgust.

"Because you guys were back together?" I ask gently.

He smiles crookedly, sighs. "Ye-ah, okay. I knew you picked up on that at the funeral. No, we weren't actually back together. But I think we would have been? If—" He breaks off, then says, "I always felt like Wendy and me had something special. And that it ended way too soon."

I want him to keep talking, so I nod.

Encouraged, he tells me, "Right before she died, me and Wendy were talking a lot. About life, you know? She was getting tired of the whole party scene. Wild Wendy—that wasn't her anymore. We had something real, but she'd never had that before, and it was hard for her to trust it. I think she was scared I would dump her like all the other guys—so she dumped me first. I mean, that's what I think."

Ellis does a long exhale. "So when her mom acted like we were still together, I didn't think it was the best time to say, 'Well, actually, she broke up with me.'"

"Right," I agree, even as I wonder how I can ask about the stuff Wendy put on her Facebook page.

He must see the confusion on my face, because he says abruptly, "That whole Nico thing was a joke. She never meant any of it."

"Really." I can't even pretend to believe this.

"No." Irritated, he shakes his head. "Yeah, Wendy and Nico got together a few times over the summer. But that was it. 'Don't believe the hype' was what she said. People just loved talking about it because it gave them a chance to bash her. I told the detective that, but I could see he didn't believe me."

"Well, there was the whole Facebook thing," I say softly. "Wendy did say she liked Nico."

"Okay, she put it out there. You know why? Because Sasha was a bitch to her," Ellis says sharply. "Wendy liked annoying her. Her so-called passion for Nico was a total scam. Pretty funny, really. When you think about it."

He trails off, and I wonder if he knows how desperate he sounds. Then he bursts out with "You know, people at this school are seriously effed up. Like they decide who you are—based on nothing—and who you should be with, and if you break their rules, the punishment is . . ."

The emotion is too much. It wells up in his eyes, and in his throat, choking off his words. I take a step toward him, wanting to say, "Yeah, I get it, I know exactly what you mean." But then I see Lindsey running up the path.

"Hey, hey, hey . . ." Taking Ellis by the arm, she says firmly, "Breathe. You are not breathing."

"I'm okay," he says.

"Uh-huh. Come on." She starts leading him away.

At first, Ellis doesn't say anything, just stumbles down the path beside her. Then all of a sudden, he calls over his shoulder, "I'm sorry, Rain."

I shake my head, even as I wonder, What is he apologizing for now?

Behind me, I hear Taylor say, "I leave you alone with a man for ten minutes and you turn him into a basket case. What is your secret?"

"We were talking about Wendy," I say, watching Ellis disappear. "He thought they were getting back together."

Taylor sighs. "Love *is* blind."

As we continue through the park, I keep watching Ellis and Lindsey. I ask Taylor, "Speaking of which, is Lindsey hot for Ellis, does she have a big-sister complex—what?"

She shrugs. "They've been friends since they were six."

"Does Lindsey even do the guy thing?"

Taylor thinks. "Never seen her do the girl thing. It's always been Lindsey and Ellis."

Which is true. In fact, Ellis's name used to come up whenever people did the "gay or no" game at parties, because any guy who's smart and good-looking and has a girl as a best friend—gay, of course. Kids used to call them the Amazing Ambiguous Duo.

Then he started dating Wendy and that stopped.

"Swings," says Taylor. Jolted out of my thoughts about Ellis, I shake my head. "All, most, or few?"

Our assignment. The thing we're supposed to be thinking about. Right.

"Ah—all. Anybody can use the swings."

"There's a weight limit," says Taylor smugly. "No fat kids. No grown-ups."

"Most," I say, through gritted teeth.

"Really?" Taylor looks over at the swing set. "I see six kids on the swings. How many kids do you think *want* to be on those swings?"

I look at the crowd hanging around the fence, even on this grisly day. "So, you wait your turn. You *share*."

"People don't always wait their turn. Sometimes it's hard to share."

Taylor's saying something else here. I look at her.

Shrugging, she says, "You were Wendy's friend, you should know."

Social studies is the last class of the day. It's growing dark as Ms. Wilentz dismisses us. A group leaves with her to return to school, Lindsey and Ellis among them. Ellis will have chess,

Lindsey volleyball. Friends leave with friends. Other kids wander off on their own.

Taylor and I walk to Central Park West. Taylor says, "Hey, I need major help on an English paper. I am not getting the Romantics. At. All. I start reading and just . . . gag."

English. The Romantics. Mr. Farrell, I think dreamily. God, I'd love to be in that class—although I'd just swoon the whole time.

"I think I can help you," I say solemnly.

"Excellent. Tomorrow? Coffee date? We'll discuss—gak—poetry?" I nod. "Awesome." She kisses me on the cheek. "And now I am late for a newspaper meeting. Bye."

She runs off, leaving me alone by the park wall. Wondering, Did Ellis kill Wendy?

My gut says no. But my gut also says he's lying about something.

In the chill air, I hear clear and sharp, "Hey."

I turn, see Lindsey charging toward me.

I have always liked Lindsey. Or, rather, the idea of Lindsey; I don't know her that well. She's smart, tough, allergic to crap. So it's a little disturbing to see her headed in my direction, fists clenched and looking fierce.

"What the hell?" she barks, stopping right in front of me.

I try to keep my voice steady. "What the hell what, Lindsey?"

"What the hell were you doing? Like, it isn't a crappy enough day for Ellis, coming here? What's with the ambush? Why'd you have to talk about her?"

There's an edge of crazy in Lindsey's voice.

"He didn't seem to mind talking about Wendy."

"Of course not," says Lindsey. "He never fricking stops talking about her."

"Well, I guess he loved her," I say quietly.

That seems to douse the anger. Lindsey sighs, "I guess so."

She stares at the buildings across the street. Her eyes are full of tears. This isn't a battle anymore.

In a soft voice, she says, "I never liked her. But what happened was evil." She breathes harshly. "That violent scumbag."

This is not acting. Lindsey absolutely believes Nico killed Wendy.

Wanting her take on Wendy and Ellis's relationship, I say, "I know you didn't love Wendy—and I totally get why. But I liked her with Ellis. I was sorry they broke up." As casually as possible, I add, "Ellis said they were maybe getting back together."

"Yeah," says Lindsey slowly. "He's always been one for fantasy."

"Wouldn't Ellis know?" I ask.

"Let's just say he has reasons for wanting to believe that."

She doesn't look at me while she speaks, preoccupied by whatever it is she's not telling me. I press, "What reasons?"

Startled, she stammers, "It's hard to let go."

"But they only dated for a little while," I say.

She blows a stray curl out of her eyes. "She was his first girlfriend, okay?"

"So?"

Impatient, she says, "So, there are things he doesn't know. Things he doesn't want to know," she adds quietly.

"About Wendy?"

"About himself. Things that Wendy helped him ignore. Things he wants to ignore because his mom and dad will totally freak if he can't."

She widens her eyes at me: Want me to spell it out?

I remember Ellis's ranting. *All these stupid rules of how people should be and who loves who.* I flash back on times I saw Ellis and Wendy together. How sweet they were, how fun. They were always laughing, and I thought, That's good for her. Someone who can be a friend.

There's my answer. What Ellis was lying about. Why he insisted, in spite of all the evidence, that he and Wendy were getting back together.

"Things like being gay," I say.

Lindsey nods. "Wendy was already pretty far out as far as his parents were concerned. They're sweet, smart people, but they come from a very conservative part of India. Gay is not going to work for them. And making Mom and Dad happy is priority number one for Ellis."

"Did Wendy know he was gay? Was that why she ended it?"

"She didn't say so, but come on. I give her credit," says Lindsey. "After they broke up, she could have been stupid, gone around whispering and giggling. 'Oooh, he's gay.' But she never made it about him. I didn't expect that."

"Wendy knew about judging. She wouldn't do that to someone she cared about."

But it's a surprise to me, too. Wendy, it turns out, was better at keeping secrets than I realized.

So, there's one lie explained. But I still want to know where Ellis was the night Wendy died.

"Were you at Karina's party that night?" I ask Lindsey.

"Not my crowd." She smiles tightly. "Ellis likes them, thinks they're funny."

"But he didn't go either."

"Nope. We did the movie and dinner thing. Wendy had made

it clear that she was going to try and get with Nico. He didn't want to see that mess."

The picture's getting clearer and clearer. Still, I have to ask, "Does Ellis have cuff links?"

"Cuff links?" Lindsey looks startled. "Who wears cuff links?"

"I found one in the hallway the other day," I lie. "Had an E on it. Or maybe it's a ring, I couldn't tell. I thought maybe Ellis's parents got them?"

She shakes her head. "Ellis isn't his name. It's Roshan. He came up with Ellis, thinks it makes him sound more prep."

My turn to be startled. "Are you serious?"

"Totally. If I want to piss him off, I call him Roshan." She grins. "Someday, I swear: Roshan Patel will get it that he is supremely cool the way he is."

I think of Wendy, how I waited for her to understand that she was a cool person without all the guy drama—and when she didn't, I pulled away. "You're a good friend, Lindsey."

Surprised, she smiles. "Thanks. Can I ask?"

"What?"

"Why so curious about all this?"

"Just trying to be a good friend too," I tell her.

DAY ELEVEN

The next day, I'm supposed to have my Romantics meeting with Taylor after school. That afternoon, she texts me: In Garden. Meet @ 4?

The Garden, I wonder. What's Taylor doing in the Garden? Then I remember: The student art show.

The student art show has been hung in a space called the Garden, a huge, airy atrium that stands between the front lobby and the administrative offices. Only, this week, instead of plants and flowers, there's art. Paintings suspended from the ceiling, delicate pottery poised on pedestals. And sculpture, of course.

As I walk through the lobby, I look at the pictures of graduating classes from the past. I slow down as I pass 1995, Mr. Farrell's year. I find his name among the many—T. H. Farrell—then search the rows of tiny faces for his.

"Not you, too."

I turn, embarrassed. Taylor is standing behind me, eyebrow raised.

"What?" I say.

Taylor rolls her eyes, coos, "'Oh, Mr. Farrell—could you explain Tennyson to me?' 'Oh, Mr. Farrell, I simply adore Goethe.' Every chick I know lusts after that guy."

Her casual scorn hits me hard. I am burning with anger and humiliation; I can't even look at Taylor. I have never told her about my crush on Mr. Farrell. She's so harsh with romantic issues, it never felt safe. Now I'm glad.

With the one thin thread of rationality I have right now, I tell myself I shouldn't be surprised that lots of girls like Mr. Farrell. He's gorgeous.

Trying to sound casual, I say, "He's cute in that teacher way."

Taylor shakes her head. "I so don't see it. I can't stand the way people drool over him."

"He can't help that," I point out, not sure if I'm defending him or myself.

"I don't know." Taylor frowns. "I . . ."

But she stops. Then says abruptly, "I have to review the student art show. Then we can talk."

Relieved by the switch in subject, I follow her into the Garden. Stopping by a clay pot, she gets out her notebook. "I hate art. Nobody gives anything a real name, because if they told you what it was supposed to be, you'd say, Oh, that's crap. So it's all Mood Number Six. Memory Number One Thirty-Nine. Or whatever." She points at the pot with her pencil. "I mean, what do I say about this?"

"Um—delicate? Nice colors?"

Taylor nods approvingly, writes it down. "Sorry, I'll make a few notes, then we can go."

"I can wait," I tell her.

While I do, I look at the rest of the work. And yes, I am drawn to Sasha's piece. Partly because it's far and away the best thing in the room and partly because . . .

Well, just because.

I approach quietly, as if it's Sasha herself. It's a slender, winding coil—a ribbon spinning in air or . . . a body. Yep, I think, a female body spiraling gracefully, happy in her freedom. No face, no obvious clues. Just there. Undeniable.

There's a little card on the pedestal. Usually they have the name of the student and whatever they want to tell you. A title or why they did it.

#14. Sasha Meloni. No title, of course.

Then I notice another line in the corner.

For my grandmother, Eleanora.

Eleanora, I think, uneasily.

Then: So what? I love my grandmother, Sasha loves hers. Wowsie zowsie.

But that's not it. Grandmothers give their things to their children and grandchildren. Things like pictures. Jewelry.

I feel Taylor behind me. She whispers, "Hey—no knocking over Sasha's stuff."

"Eleanora," I say without meaning to.

"Ye-es?"

Sasha's fingers in the clay, strong, shaping, digging, tearing.

She was pathetic. She was a liar. She had no life, so she tried to steal other people's.

Sasha kicking me. Hitting me. A Sasha I'd never seen before.

Of course, if the boyfriend you killed someone over looked like he was going to jail for a crime you committed—that could stress you out.

"Rain?"

"I totally forgot, I have something I need to do," I tell Taylor. "I'll make it up to you, promise."

* * *

I should tell Mr. Farrell.

Or my mom.

Or Detective Vasquez.

I mean, someone should know I'm going to Nico Phelps's house.

He was calm when I called. As if he expected this.

"I know something," I told him.

"Oh, yeah?" Bored, no interest. Because hey, nothing I knew could be important.

"It could help."

"Okay."

"But I have questions. And you might not want to answer those questions in front of your lawyers."

I said I wanted to meet in a coffee shop. He said he didn't like to go out. For a moment, we were stuck.

Then he said sarcastically, "My mom is here, you don't have to worry."

Now I think, I could be setting up a date with a killer, but it's okay because, hey, his mom will be there.

You have to take two buses to get to where Nico Phelps lives, way down in the Thirties, over on the East Side. I don't know the neighborhood well. I've only been to movies here once or twice.

Nico's building is modern, but not stylish modern. Red brick with little balconies on every floor. The doorman raises an eyebrow when I say Phelps.

When I ring the bell, it's Mrs. Phelps who answers the door. She holds it only partly open. She is a small woman, with a sharp, tired face and short, ragged gray hair. One lock stands up, and

175

I have the feeling she pulls on it. She's wearing sneakers and a faded dress that's been put through the wash too many times.

She looks like the maid, I think, an exhausted, old woman.

She also looks suspicious. I guess I'm not the kind of girl Nico hangs out with.

"I don't know you, do I?" she says. The voice is a lot stronger than her appearance. When she talks, she expects to be listened to.

"Hi, Mrs. Phelps. Rain Donovan. I go to Nico's school?" She shakes her head; that doesn't matter to her. "Is he not here?" I ask tentatively.

She glances down. The hand moves up the doorjamb; I can tell, she's thinking of letting me in. "What is this about?"

"I need to talk to him. I . . . I think . . ."

I'm about to say I think I can help when Nico appears at the door and pulls it open. "Ma, it's okay." To me, he says, "Come in."

The apartment he leads me into is small. A tiny, very clean kitchen is right off the entryway. Nico leads me through a living room with a thick rug on the carpet. Heavy, dark furniture, awkward and old-fashioned, crowds in on you. Everywhere you look, pictures of Nico. Fat baby Nico. Little boy Nico at the beach. Nico in a suit outside a church. I try to feel his father in the house. I can't.

A short, narrow hallway takes us to Nico's room. There is only one bedroom; his mom must sleep in the living room. I can feel her watching from the kitchen. "Remember what the lawyer said," she calls just before Nico closes the door.

And I am alone in a room with Nico Phelps.

I look around, wondering where to sit. It's a medium-sized

room, but there's a ton of stuff crammed into it. Nico's bureau is crowded with all kinds of product; there's a strong smell of Marc Jacobs cologne. The blinds on the window are closed. The bed is not made. The door to the closet is open, and I can see Nico's mass of designer clothes, his shirts and ties and pairs and pairs of shoes. In the corner, a TV is going without sound. I'm startled to see it's the news. Nico's laptop sits open on the bed. Peeking, I see he's been reading an article about the case. He's streaming a radio station. I hear "And the latest developments in—" before he switches off the sound. His eyes linger on the screen for a moment, drinking in the last details of the article before he snaps the laptop shut.

"You're following the news?" I ask. He nods. "Doesn't it freak you out?"

He shrugs. "Gotta see what they're saying, right?" He throws himself onto the bed and lounges. He's dressed in sweatpants and a T-shirt. The fabric is tight through the shoulders and biceps; I'd forgotten how big he is. How strong. By the bed, there is a big picture of him and Sasha. They're lying entwined on the grass. Sweet, I think automatically, most guys wouldn't do that. Except I notice she's staring off into the distance, wearing sunglasses. Nico's looking the other way. Two beautiful profiles. It's a Ralph Lauren ad.

"Take off your coat," he says.

It's not a request. I take it off.

"I'm not going to hurt you," says Nico contemptuously.

No? I think. You probably don't think you hurt me that time in the stairwell. You probably think it was no big thing.

Folding my arms, I sit on the edge of the desk chair.

"You wanted to talk," he says.

"Yeah."

"All of a sudden, you like to talk."

Sensing a trap, I shake my head.

"Like you talked to the cops."

I feel a desperate need to apologize, to throw up a wall of I'm sorry before he lets loose with rage.

Then, suddenly I'm calm, almost chilly. I don't have to apologize to Nico Phelps.

"I thought you killed her."

"And now?"

"Not sure."

He shifts slightly. I have made him uncomfortable. Good, I think.

"You said you knew something," he says. "That could maybe help."

I nod. "But I need to know something before I tell you."

"Like what?"

Like did Sasha kill Wendy? Yeah, right. I'll lose him entirely if I start that way.

Instead I say, "Like what really happened between you and Wendy that night."

He rolls his eyes. This is a guy who seriously resents having to do things for other people. "Why should I tell you?"

"Because what I know is important." I see him hesitate. "It would change things, I promise."

"Oh, I guess you feel guilty," he sneers.

"No. But Wendy was my friend."

"And obviously I killed her," he says sarcastically.

"Would you tell me if you did?"

"Yeah, I *didn't*."

Nico's been saying these words his whole life, I think. They're the same words he gave the cops when they busted him for drugs over the summer. Same words he gave to teachers who accused him of cheating. Same words he probably gave to his mom when she asked if he stole twenty bucks from her wallet.

"Will you tell me the whole thing?" I ask. "Everything that happened that night?"

"Sure." He shrugs again. *Who cares? Whatever.*

"Even things you just felt, but didn't necessarily know?"

That surprises him. "Sure." He pulls at a thread on the blanket. "One thing I felt? Thought, whatever? There was something going on with Wendy that night," he says softly. "Something weird."

He hesitates, then blurts out, "So you know the whole deal, how we got together a few times in summer?" I nod. "Then this year, I'm with Sasha and Wendy's like, I'm not letting go. You're mine. We're trashy. We belong together. But she was funny about it, you know? No big deal. I kind of thought it was a game, almost."

There's something important there. I file the word *game* in my brain.

He sighs. "Then I start hearing about the Facebook thing. And like . . . that was a little much."

"Did Sasha have a problem with it?" I ask.

"Not that she said, but all of a sudden I was getting a lot of static about other things. I'm sure it bugged her."

That scans. I say, "So, that night . . ."

He crosses his arms, looks toward the TV. In a rush, he says, "That night I left the party to hook up with Wendy." He gives me a *You happy now?* grimace.

"But you weren't going to end it with Sasha?"

"Hell, no."

"I don't get it."

"Like I said, Sasha'd been giving me a lot of grief. 'You need to focus. Grow up, don't drink.' Stuff about my mom. Kind of like, 'If you're going to be one of us . . .'" He shrugs. "I liked Wendy. She was cute, sexy. She wasn't going to get you anywhere special in life. . . ."

In other words, not connected. When you're shooting for Brown, you want a girl who can lend you her E pin to wear on college interviews.

Then Nico says, "Anyway, I wanted a break."

"And Wendy was the break."

He nods. "So, we're talking at the party, and I'm like, Yeah, cool, let's do it. That's when she starts with the demands. Starts pushing real hard for us to leave together—like that moment."

"What'd you do?"

"I told her we couldn't leave together, but that I'd leave right after her. She wasn't happy, but she accepted that. Then when she was gone, I waited ten, fifteen minutes. Made sure Sash wasn't around. Then I left."

His face is bland, his voice casual. Lying to the girl you're lying to your girlfriend about, I think. Wow.

"Where did you meet?"

"On the corner. By the newsstand."

"What were you guys going to do?" I ask.

"We were going to go to her house. Her mom wasn't home. And it was close."

I think. Karina lives in the upper Eighties, Wendy in the low Seventies. Not that close. Not close enough for them to have made it to her apartment and have Nico back at the party that fast.

"But you didn't go."

He shakes his head.

"You changed your mind."

"No—*she* changed her mind."

Surprised, I say, "Excuse me?"

"Seriously," he says. "She flipped out on me."

"What do you mean?"

He frowns, irritated by the memory. "Like I said, I waited to leave the party. Because I didn't want people thinking—"

"That what was happening was actually happening," I say.

"Yeah. So when I finally meet her, she's totally pissed. Like, Where were you? You kept me waiting. All this crap. And I'm drunk, not thinking. So I say, It's fine, nobody saw me leave. But of course, she's such a drama queen, she wants everyone to know everything. So she got all snotty with me, like, Oh, well, thank *God* nobody saw you leave, because that would be the end of the world, right? She kept asking me: Was I sure, how was I so sure? Somebody must have seen me. And I got mad and yelled, No, nobody saw me. 'Cause I was *careful*. And I guess that pissed her off even more because that's when she really lost it. Starts hitting me." He waves his fists weakly in the air, lets out a little *Eeehhh*, an imitation of a girl fighting.

"What'd you do?"

"I laughed, to be honest. Then it got annoying and I held her hands. That's when she broke free and scratched me." He holds up his hands and I see the faint lines.

That explains why they found Nico's skin under Wendy's nails. "What then?"

Nico thinks. "She's screaming at me, 'You all think you can just keep handing me crap and I'll keep eating it, well, I won't, blah, blah . . .'"

Something strikes me. "'You all'? What, you and Sasha?"

He sighs. "All men, who knows. She said she was tired of being a secret."

It almost makes sense. The school mattress hating guys she gives it up to. Only, Wendy was never a secret. Everything she did—every guy she stole—it was all out in the open. She certainly wasn't a secret with Ellis. And her Nico obsession couldn't have been more public. But I guess this time she wanted more than the bathroom. She wanted Nico to make a big statement to Sasha and all the snobs who looked down on her by leaving with her. To tell the world she was a real girlfriend now. And when he didn't, she was pissed.

Then Nico says, "So, I said I was sorry. 'Cause by then I was tired and not really up for drama."

"What'd you say? Exactly?"

He pauses, concentrating. "I told her, 'Okay, I get it, I'm sorry. Let's call it off.'" He looks away. "I felt a little bad. I had told her things weren't cool with Sasha. Maybe I let her think . . . I don't know."

"And what'd she say when you said sorry, let's not do this?"

Nico nods as he remembers. "This was weird. One second, she's scratching me, screaming at me. Next minute, she's totally cool."

"What?"

"Yeah. Once I said forget it, she just laughed."

"Laughed?"

"Yeah. Cheered right up. Even said she was sorry for the

scratches." He sees I don't believe him. "Seriously. She gave me a kiss on the cheek and said 'Bye, lover man.' Walked off all happy."

"She was putting on a show."

"Nope. She was happy."

Impatient, I say, "No offense, Nico, but how would you know? I don't get the sense you spent a lot of time worrying about Wendy's feelings."

"You weren't the only one who got Wendy," he says slowly. "The whole pool cleaner thing, I could relate to that. Maybe you don't know this"—a nasty glint in his eye tells me he's being sarcastic—"but some people can't get over the fact that my mom's a nurse. Or that we used to live in Queens. Wendy and me used to talk about that, how full of it people were at school. How weird it was to be with these kids who'd never been anything but rich, had no clue any other life existed."

I don't think Nico's lying. "Bye, lover man." That's pure Wendy. Nico couldn't invent that.

So, why would Wendy tell the guy she supposedly wanted more than anything to get lost?

That whole Nico thing was just a joke. She never meant any of it. 'Don't believe the hype' was what she said.

Remembering Ellis's words, I say, "This is a weird question. . . ."

"Yeah, I'm charged with murder, so ask."

"Do you think Wendy was ever really into you?"

His mouth quirks up. "What, did she truly 'love' me or was it a status thing or—"

"No. I mean, did you ever feel she was making more of it than it was? Almost on purpose? As if people *knowing* she liked you was more important than—"

"She was pretty needy in the attention department," Nico points out.

"Yeah, and she liked annoying girls like Sasha. But this seems different. Even more out there."

Wendy setting down her drink. *Could you 'scoose me?*

"She even made a big show of letting me know," I realize. "And then . . ."

"What?" says Nico tensely.

"And then she tells you to get lost. When she had made it so public that she was going to get you. I mean, why not at least take the scalp?"

Nico says slowly, "You think the whole thing was a scam to cover for something else?"

I nod. "When I was friends with Wendy, she used to tell her mom she was with me when she wanted to sneak out to parties. Using one person to cover for something else—she knew how to do that. She was mad when no one saw you because she wanted people to think you guys were together. And then she needed to get rid of you without making you suspicious."

Nico shows me his hands. "She was pretty seriously mad."

"Sure," I say simply. "You weren't very nice to her. But I don't think you were the point of that evening."

"So she gets rid of me so she can meet this other guy without people knowing." He shakes his head. "So, she met this guy in the park and then what?"

"I don't know." I shudder. "I don't know."

But Nico can see a way out now. Excited, he demands, "Who else was she into?"

"You're thinking the person she was meeting was the person who killed her," I point out.

"Kind of obvious."

"Is it? Where was Sasha?"

He turns his head sharply, wrinkles his nose. "Come on. . . ."

"Wendy got a kick out of annoying her, you admitted it, I can tell you personally Sasha has a temper. She's not afraid to get physical. Maybe your little game with Wendy wasn't so funny to her."

"Then she'd kick *my* ass," he says simply. "She has before."

"Do you know for a fact she stayed at the party while you were gone? Maybe she followed you."

"What, then followed Wendy to the park so she could kill her? I'm not worth all that."

"You're not, but her pride is. Sasha's got a lot of it; haven't you noticed? Or maybe she just lost it. She didn't have to plan on killing Wendy, just let her have it. Everyone was waiting for that—when would Sasha kick Wendy's ass?"

He's silent.

"Maybe it just went too far."

He leans forward, puts his chin on his fist. "I don't see it," he says finally.

"You don't want to."

"Believe me," he says, "I'd be real happy to find someone else to pin this on. But it's not Sash."

"If it is, they'll find out," I warn him. "Someone will have noticed she left."

"She didn't leave. And she didn't do it. Leave her out of this, I'm serious."

He's shouting now. And he's almost off the bed. I gasp, pull myself in tight.

A knock at the door. Nico's mom calls his name. Her voice is gentle, as if she knows he's in trouble.

Nico settles right down. Says, "Yeah, Mom, I'm fine."

When he's sure she's gone, he says in a calmer voice, "Anyway, a girl couldn't have done that."

"Wendy wasn't that big," I remind him.

He looks at me. "Maybe the person she was meeting did it. Only maybe she wasn't meeting a guy."

It takes me a moment to get what Nico is saying. "Come on."

He shakes his head. "Maybe Wendy got tired of the guy thing. She used to joke about it. 'Women are so much cooler than men, why do I waste my time?' Only maybe she was with somebody who wasn't so into people knowing she was gay. Maybe that's who was keeping her a secret. Maybe they had a fight about it."

Nico is relaxed now, shoulders comfortable, feet up. He's looking right at me.

It's almost funny.

"Are you serious?"

He shrugs. "I'm way off?"

"Way, way."

"You have an alibi?"

I don't, as a matter of fact, which is weird. I was probably home or on my way home when Wendy was killed. The doorman was off duty. My mom was asleep. No one knows when I got in.

As lightly as possible, I say, "What, you're going to pin this on me?"

"You say anything about Sasha, I just might."

I'm about to say, Yeah, Nico, I think you're going to have a problem getting people to believe that. Shy, no-life, always-listens-to-others gal, a killer? Not to mention you don't have a shred of proof.

But then I remember that picture of myself from freshman year. How angry I looked. It was a surprise to me, that I put that much rage out there. But maybe it wouldn't be such a surprise to other people.

In a softer voice, I ask, "Have you seen Sasha since . . ." It seems rude to mention his arrest.

He gazes at his closet full of clothes. "We talk on the phone, but her parents are talking about sending her abroad for the summer, maybe even sooner if they can work it out with the school."

Which would get her away from Nico, I think. But also get her away from the police.

It's hard for me not to see Nico as a jerk. But I try to see him as a human being who needs help when I say, "Nico, you know Sasha really well. Seriously. You think there's no way she did this?"

"No way," he says firmly.

"Even if you go to jail?"

He's silent. Then says, "You said you knew something that could help me."

I look at him. He's tensed up since we started talking about Sasha. No more lolling around on the bed. Now he's sitting hunched and anxious, elbows on knees, hands gripped tight together.

I say, "Have the cops talked to you about a pin?"

I catch a wave of shame; Nico takes a deep breath, then nods. "Yeah, they said they found one of the school pins near Wendy. At first I was like, I don't have one, you can check. Then they said, Yeah, we know your girlfriend gave you hers. I didn't want them hassling Sash, so I admitted that she did give me one. That I wanted it for college stuff, to wear on interviews."

"I don't get that: wouldn't the college check with the school?"

"People look at the surface. If they like what they see, they don't ask questions."

Okay. "So what happened to the pin?"

"I lost it. I told the cops, but amazingly, they don't believe me."

I don't either. "What happened to it, Nico?"

He ducks his head. "Okay. I didn't lose it. I . . . there was this girl. At a bar. Said she had modeling connects. We were both fairly high." He smiles bitterly. "She wanted it. I gave it to her."

"Wow."

"Yeah."

"Tried asking for it back?"

"She was Italian. Gabriella something. The lawyer's working on it. Stupid bitch really screwed me up."

This is how Nico sees life, I realize. In his universe, all the things that go wrong for him—not his fault. These crazy women just keep screwing things up for him. I open my mouth, ready to demand how he can treat Sasha so badly when he actually does care about her. Then I remember Wendy. How every guy she went after was tied up with some girl she hated. Romance, rejection, and revenge—it was all tangled up for her. No wonder she understood Nico.

Do I really want to help this guy?

No. But in the end, Nico doesn't matter. It's about me making what I said right.

"The E pin," I say. "The one the police say they have. Ask for a picture. It's not what Sasha gave you and you can prove it."

He straightens up. "Seriously?"

I nod.

"Thanks." He says the word slowly, as if it's a foreign word and he's not sure he's pronouncing it right.

I stand up, raise my hand in good-bye. Nico does the same, staying on the bed.

For a moment, we look at each other, both thinking the same thing.

Nico says, "I guess you were kind of pissed at me. That's why you called the cops."

His voice is casual, as if my anger is no big deal to him.

"I called the cops," I say, imitating his casual tone, "because of a lot of things. Including the fact you've got a serious mean streak."

Nico nods slowly. "Yeah, I figured it was because of what happened."

"It didn't *happen*," I say harshly. "It was something you *did*."

This, he hears. His mouth bunches up, like a sulky kid's. He waves his hand, part apology, part whatever.

"Why did you do that?" I ask. "I've never gotten it."

"It was a joke," he says lazily.

"No, it wasn't. You picked me. Why?"

He sighs. Shrugging, he says, "That place is weird, man. Alcott. Like, everybody's rich, everybody's already chosen, you know? The good life is already in place, laid out in front of them." He shrugs. "Just sometimes, I felt like a freak, you know?"

"So, you found a bigger freak and humiliated her? No, I don't know."

He looks up. "One day, I overheard some chick saying how you had this weird thing where you were born with a hole in your mouth and didn't talk right. She said she felt sorry for you. It pissed me off." He ducks his head, embarrassed.

"Why?"

"I don't know. I was like, Yeah, *her* they feel sorry for. Me—no way. 'Cause I'm a guy and . . ." He gestures around the room, reminding me of its smallness and cheapness. "Something could be wrong with you and it was okay. I watched you, the way you scurried around, like you were always about to burst into tears. I thought you felt sorry for yourself. Wanted me to feel sorry for you. And it just made me mad."

It's almost funny, Nico feeling oppressed by me. I think of telling him about retard and deaf girl, about Rain, Rain, go away. About being terrified to speak to the people standing right next to you. About feeling alone.

But I think Nico knows what that's like.

"It wasn't okay," I tell him. "Not for a long time. You know who made it better?" He looks up, knowing what I'm about to say. "Wendy."

"She was cool," he says.

"That she was." I take a step toward the door. I've said all the things that matter to Nico; he's said all the things that matter to me.

Except one. I turn, ask, "Seriously. No way Sasha did it?"

"No way."

But he doesn't look at me as he says it.

That night, there is a full-hour special on the case on TV. I know some kids from school are in it. The crews have been filming around the building, but Dorland wouldn't let them inside, of course. My mom is out performing, so I can watch it without sighs and eye rolls.

They start with the playground where Wendy was found.

Show little kids shrieking as they go down the slide, flying high on the swings. Then a big low chord, cut to the green space with yellow tape all around it. Then the shots of Nico being arrested.

"Wendy Geller," the narrator intones solemnly as a big picture of Wendy comes up. "Nico Phelps." A picture of Nico scowling in his pseudomodel pose comes up beside it. "A date with death!"

"Wendy Geller and Nico Phelps. Two privileged members of an exclusive New York club of the young and wealthy. They went to the right clubs"—a shot of Wendy at some bar—"knew the right people"—a shot of Sasha and Nico getting off a private plane. "But on the night of November eighth, something went terribly wrong."

A swirl of images. Baby Wendy, little girl Wendy, Wendy on a swing in her backyard in Long Island. Baby Nico. Nico in a Halloween costume as Batman, Nico on the beach with Wendy.

"Who was Wendy Geller? Who was Nico Phelps?" They freeze on the beach image, close in on Nico's face. A cheesy X-ray effect. "Tonight, we reveal the monster behind the mask."

Cut to Kirsty Pennington, who tells them how Nico threw a drink in her face. An interview with the cop who arrested him in the Hamptons. A priest who tells us that Nico's father has never been part of his life.

Then it's Wendy's turn. Karina fills the screen as she says, "Let me tell you, Wendy Geller was not some innocent little girl."

And there it is, the *Get You* video, as they're calling it now. Wendy crooning to the screen, "This is a message from Wendy Geller to Nico Phelps. Nico, you best be listening. Because two days from now at Karina Burroughs's party, I am going to get you. I am going to get you and you are going to love every moment."

I watch this carefully, thinking of my conversation with Nico.

Thinking about that person Wendy was going to meet. Now I realize the video feels fake. It's Wendy playing a part, the slutty girl in some TV show, the one everyone loves to hate.

Now they have a guy they call a "noted forensic expert" talking about the skin they found under Wendy's fingernails. He says, "It's actually quite easy to leave bits of our DNA around. Saliva on a cup, sweat on a steering wheel, bits of skin rubbed off on the handle of a murder weapon. We can detect DNA on a remarkably small fragment of skin, provided the sample isn't degraded."

The reporter says, "And they found Nico Phelps's DNA on the skin under Wendy Geller's fingernails."

"That is correct."

"But if it's so easy, wouldn't the DNA of other people be present as well?"

The expert smiles condescendingly. "Yes, but those people are not accused of murder."

Images all over the screen: Wendy screaming with laughter with a drink in her hand. Nico lounging on the steps of the school, looking snotty. Wendy dancing, Nico smoking. Wendy, Nico, Wendy, Nico, Wendy, Nico.

I pick up the remote, turn off the TV.

An hour later, my phone buzzes. It's a text from Taylor.

You said you'd make it up to me. Breakfast tomorrow?

DAY TWELVE–THE LAST DAY

We're sitting in the diner near school in a small booth right by the kitchen. It's the breakfast rush. Plates and pans crash and bang. Cooks and waiters shout orders back and forth. It's noisy, and I worry I won't be able to hear what Taylor has to say.

That is, if she ever speaks. Taylor is pulling her napkin apart, focused on it, like she has to get the size of the shredded pieces just right. It's strange to see her nervous. Nervous is for people who are afraid they'll do the wrong thing.

I'm nervous too. I'm supposed to be helping her with a paper, but we've been here for fifteen minutes and Taylor hasn't mentioned the Romantics yet. I get the feeling this breakfast isn't about Mr. Farrell's class, it's about Mr. Farrell.

In a rush Taylor says, "Look, this is weird, so I'm just going to say it. I know you're twisted up about Wendy."

I nod.

"And I feel like I haven't really been there for you."

"You have, Tay, more than anybody. . . ."

She shakes her head. "I haven't. And we both know why. I didn't like her."

"She wasn't your kind of person."

"No. I actually disliked her. If there'd been a person there to hate—I would have."

It's automatic now, wondering who hated Wendy, why, and how much. How would Wendy have hurt Taylor?

"Anyway," she says. "You know my class with Farrell?"

I say, "The one we're supposed to be talking about now?"

"Remember I complained about those girls who were all like, Oooh, Mr. Farrell, come look at my poetry?"

"Yeah."

"Did I mention Wendy was also in the class?"

This is a little thing, a small thing. Wendy was in the class. There are no bombs in that sentence. But my body is jolted long before my brain gets it.

I smile. "Don't tell me. She gave Farrell the Wendy treatment."

But Taylor's not going to let me joke. "Oh, yeah." Her voice is dead, flat.

"And what? Say what you need to say." My voice is not quite steady.

Now it's Taylor's turn to hesitate. "I don't have proof."

"What, Taylor? Proof of what?"

She can't meet my eye. "It was just a sense. Based on what I saw."

"What did you see?"

She looks hard to one side, as if she's staring into the past. "Little closed-door conversations after class."

Come on in . . .

I set my teeth on my tongue, make my mind go blank. No words from me until Taylor's finished. I have to hear it all.

Taylor says, "There were . . . little pats on the arm from him. I saw her rubbing his shoulders once. He looked embarrassed about that. And then one day, she was yakking away in class. Farrell says, Miss Geller. And she was like, Yes, Mr. Farrell? And he said—"

She pauses, trying to remember exactly. "He said, 'Be silent.' Or something like that. And they gave each other these little smiles, and I just thought, Yeah, it's going on."

Going on. My mind shows me what that means. Wendy and Mr. Farrell smiling. Then kissing. The shoulder rub ending as she slides onto his lap. I see his hand on her leg, see her skirt rise.

"Then a month ago, she was all sulky and acting up to get his attention. I thought, Oh, must be over."

Wendy. The girl who told everyone everything—what would she keep secret?

An affair with a married teacher. Yep, even Wendy would keep that one a secret. As much as she could. And anyone who noticed when she slipped? People like Taylor or even Karina? She'd keep them guessing by running after another guy. Someone outrageous. Someone taken. So that we'd all keep yakking about Wendy and Nico and Sasha.

And we'd totally miss what was really going on.

I'm not aware I'm standing up until Taylor says, "Rain?"

"I think I need to be somewhere else," I say with complete seriousness.

"Okay," says Taylor, gathering her bag. "Then I need to be there with you."

One thing I do know about where I'm going: Taylor can't be there. I'm about to say, No, no, please don't. But then I have a better idea. I push the check toward her. "Could you do this? I have no money."

And while she goes to the register to pay, I slip out of the diner.

On the street, it becomes very clear: I need to find Farrell.

I hurry down the street toward school. It's freezing out, a biting winter cold, and I still have my fall jacket. The frigid air burns my lungs. My jaw hurts, my nails are deep in the flesh of my palms. I don't know what I look like as I go into the lobby. A small clue: people back off right away. They see the angry girl, the girl who scowled into the camera for her freshman yearbook picture, the girl who talked to no one because she was sure everyone was out to get her.

I pull open the door to the stairwell hard, wanting to slam it against the wall.

"Oh, my."

Ms. Laredo. Clutching her manila files. The few she managed to hang on to, as most of them are all over the floor. She stares down at them, bewildered.

"I'm really sorry, Ms. Laredo." The tears start. Stupidly, I feel terrible for the files, as if they're little kids I knocked over. I crouch down, sliding them around uselessly as I try to pick them up.

Ms. Laredo puts her hand on my arm. "Dear?"

"I'm just going to—"

"Dear." All of a sudden, Ms. Laredo's voice is firm, strong. "Why don't you come into my office?"

A box of tissues. A cup of tea. Talk about Ms. Laredo's plants—"I've had this one for seven years now"—and her corgi, Sophie, named for her dentist.

I don't feel better. But I feel . . . less crazy. The sharp agony of the knife on the bone has faded. I can sit here with a polite smile and talk about corgis.

But then Ms. Laredo goes to sit behind her desk and says, "Now. Is this about Wendy or Nico? Or Wendy and Nico?"

Actually, Ms. Laredo, it's about Wendy and Mr. Farrell. And me and Mr. Farrell. By the way, did you know Mr. Farrell likes to screw around with students? You didn't? Oh, well, it's an interesting story.

Ms. Laredo deserves some kind of answer. "I guess it got to me—just all of it." Which is honest enough.

She nods. "Are you talking to anyone about it?"

I sigh. "Not really. I'm sick of it in some ways. I feel like it's all I think about."

"Then why don't you stop?" she says gently.

"Because . . ." There is a reason not to stop, there is. Only I can't remember it right now. All I can think of is, He liked her better than me. She was cuter than me, sexier than me. She had the guts to say what she wanted.

When *did* it end? I wonder. Taylor said a month ago. . . .

I can't think about this in front of Ms. Laredo. "Because it's everywhere," I say stupidly. "You can't get away from it."

Her eyes stay on me. She's not buying it. Glancing down at the files, she says, "I am not a talker myself. I value privacy. But some things must be said, if people will be hurt by the silence."

I'm very comfortable with silence, I want to tell her.

Instead, I point to the files. "Sorry I knocked these over. You want help straightening them out?"

"Oh, no, dear." She arranges them tidily on the desk. "They're just ideas for the new E pin."

In music, there are notes that tell you to listen. All by themselves, they warn the ear: it's coming, pay attention.

And when Ms. Laredo says "new E pin," I hear the first note of the question that's been forming since I found out Farrell was Wendy's secret.

"They're changing it?"

"They change it every fifteen years, dear. That way, members of the same generation of Alcott students can recognize one another." She opens a drawer in her desk, pulls out a ring. "Here's mine, from 1957. Rose gold with quartz. Rather pretty, I think. Of course, the men objected. They made the design simpler after that."

I am surprised at the calm in my voice. "Oh, yeah? What else did they do?"

"Jeweled, that was popular. A mix of metals, that was expensive. They tried wood one time, that was a disaster. After that we went back to gold and changed the enamels. A dark green one year. Maroon."

"But never silver?"

"Oh, no, they did that, too. Not too long ago, in fact."

"When, Ms. Laredo?"

Startled, she says, "Let me think now. Twenty years ago? I suppose that seems like a long time to you. Maybe it was fifteen."

Twenty, I think. Fifteen. Take someone who graduated at eighteen, add, oh, seventeen years. You get . . . thirty-five. Thirty-five works just fine.

I say, "I think I'm okay now. Thank you, Ms. Laredo."

"Are you sure, dear? Should I call your mother?"

"No." I get up. "No, I . . . I should just get to class and . . ."

"Stop thinking about it," she says warmly.

"And, really, thank you."

I don't go to class. Instead, I go to the library. To that shelf way in the back where nobody goes. Where they keep the old yearbooks. Looking at the spines, I let my fingers travel back in time. 2005, 2000, 1995 . . .

The first yearbook I look at doesn't have it.

But the second one does.

This year's recipients of the E pin
Robert McCormack
David Helpman
Tina Daniels
T. H. Farrell

The halls are crowded just before first lunch period. Kids pour out of the classrooms, desperate to eat, to breathe, to talk to their friends. The school has a whole different life to it. Noisy, crazy, safe.

I don't talk to anyone as I make my way through the crowd. Someone bumps into me. Or I bump into them. We both mutter, Sorry. Then keep going.

Some teachers go out to lunch. Some, like Mr. Farrell, eat at their desks.

On my way to his office, I pass Ms. Englander's room. Ms. Englander goes out to eat, and the room is empty. I step inside to gaze at her wall of images. I find the picture of Blue-beard's wife and step closer. It's all black, white, and rust tones, as if it were done in chalk and dried blood. The wife stands on the far left, behind the door she has opened. She wears a long white gown, her hair is a dark shadow down her back. She cannot yet see, but maybe suspects, what's beyond the door. The bodies hanging. Each in a long white dress, feet dangling, arms limp. You do not see their faces, only their dark hair.

I leave Ms. Englander's class, walk down the hall, stop when I get to Mr. Farrell's door.

He's in there. I can hear him. All I have to do is knock.

Before I do, I fix another image in my mind: Not-Wendy, what they put into that box. The bruises people tried to hide with paint and scarves. Bruises sound like a kid thing, skinned knees. Put a Band-Aid on it, it's fine. I think of the damage under the bruises. The crushed muscles, bleeding tissue. The twisted, choking pain.

What happens when someone is strangled? A few days ago, I looked it up.

When someone is strangled by hand, the airway is blocked. Blood can't flow. Fragile bones in the neck snap. There's a bone under the tongue—that can break. The tongue gets caught between the teeth, gets bitten and bruised.

Air hunger. The body gets so frantic for air, it almost goes into convulsions. Leaping and twisting to get those hands off. The brain can't get air, and gradually, everything fades, goes dark. Unconsciousness comes before death. Which, I guess, is good. Maybe you still have some hope that it won't happen. That this is not the end.

But it is the end. The worst thing happens. You die.

The larynx—your voice box—can be crushed. Which makes me wonder, could Wendy scream? Cry for help? Or did she have no voice at all at the end?

Can I say something? Most people? Myself included? Talk way too much.

I half smile at the memory. Then think, If Wendy could, she'd scream her killer's name so the whole world heard her. She'd put it on Facebook, tell all her friends, spray-paint it in Times Square. She'd shriek till her voice was raw. But she can't. Her killer took her voice away.

So I have to use mine.

My heart is jumping, my fingers are cold. I go long stretches without breathing, then gulp for air.

I knock, hear, "Come in."

I open the door. Mr. Farrell looks startled. "Rain . . ."

He is still beautiful, and for a moment, I think, No. Wrong. I'm just crazy. This whole thing has made me crazy. I see killers everywhere.

Then I remember Mr. Farrell saying, *"Nico worries me."*

How, that very first day when I talked to him about the killing, he brought up Nico's name, even though he claimed to have no idea Wendy was nuts about Nico. How he wanted me to tell him anything I heard about the case. How he insisted I go to the police. Even called them for me, stood by me the whole time, just to make sure I told them exactly what he wanted me to.

And when I said I thought I might be wrong about Nico, he . . .

All those signals, all those clues. I saw them, heard them. I just didn't understand.

He glances at the door, then says, "You should probably shut that."

There are people outside, I think as I close the door. Still, I stay standing by the door, my hands behind my back.

"You said I should come to you," I tell him. "If I found out anything." My voice is calm, steady.

Shoving back in his chair, he says, "If you found out something that implicated someone other than Nico, yes."

At first, his tone is all impatience, dislike. He wants to frighten me with disapproval.

But then he switches, says with kindness, "By now, I'm hoping you understand better what I said. You see I'm right—"

"Oh, I do," I say, seizing the chance. "You were right—about one thing. It was an E pin they found near Wendy."

I pause.

"Your E pin."

He laughs slightly. "My—" Then he looks sad. "Oh, Rain."

"I know you have one. It says so in the yearbook."

"I . . ." He raises his hands, drops them into his lap. "I do have one, yes."

"Where is it?"

"I don't wear it because it's a meaningless status symbol."

"Bring it in tomorrow, then. Show me."

"I don't have the first idea where it is."

"I think you do. I think you know that it's your E pin the police have. The one they found near Wendy's body, the one she pulled off your finger when she tried to pry your hands off her neck before she died."

He shakes his head. "Rain, I don't know what you think you know, but you have to understand . . ."

I have done well up till now. I have been cold, detached, as if this is all happening to someone else. But when Farrell says

202

again that I have to understand—as if I could understand—I say rapidly, "No, I actually do *not* have to understand. There is no understanding what you did. Okay? Here's what I do understand. I understand that Wendy is dead. And you're alive. That means her life is over. She rots. While you get to talk to people, to hug your son. You get to breathe, to eat food—"

He turns his head abruptly. "I *don't* eat," he says quietly. "I don't sleep."

He rubs his eyes, gestures to a chair. "Sit down."

"No."

"What are you thinking, Rain?"

"That I should leave. Now. Leave and tell someone."

I reach for the doorknob. He stares—*I see you, Rain. I think about you.*

I turn the knob, pull the door open.

"No, wait—" He holds up his hand. I let the door gently swing shut.

Mr. Farrell doesn't speak right away. His briefcase is on the table, and he opens it. The picture of his little boy with his bright, loving eyes is still there. He stares at it a long while. Then he slowly closes the lid.

He whispers, "Before you . . . do anything, will you listen? Please?"

And I can't say no. After all, I am a listener. I take my hand off the knob, nod.

He sighs deeply, exhaling. "I come from a family of achievers, Rain. Professors, writers, legal scholars. To simply be like everyone else is not enough. Remember," he says in a voice from far away, "that time in the diner? When I told you I only had eyes for the girls I couldn't have?"

I swallow. "Yes."

"That was my life here. When I was a student at Alcott. I can't tell you how many times, how many girls . . ." He looks at me and I know what he's talking about. The days you come to school, hoping just to see that person. The joy when you get a chance to talk to them. The dreams you have about them.

"I didn't speak to a single one of those girls," he says. "In fact, I don't think I spoke to more than five people the entire time I went to school. Nothing beyond the empty 'Hi' or 'Sure, you can borrow my notes.' I was terrified of getting it wrong. Of giving it away that I was . . . wrong." He smiles sadly. "That's what we all think, isn't it? In school? That we're the only ones who aren't . . . right, somehow? We keep silent because we're worried that one wrong word will give it away."

I look at the empty walls, remembering how I thought it was so cool that he didn't slap up a bunch of pictures like the other teachers. He kept it clean, pure. Now I know why. He was afraid he might pick the wrong ones, reveal himself. The blankness isn't openness; it's a mask.

He sits back. "Wendy wasn't like that, was she? Frightened? Worried? She did exactly what she wanted, never seemed to care about what people thought." He looks at me. "That's why we wanted to be near her, as if we could learn."

He wants you on his side, I tell myself. He's trying to make you feel that you and he are alike.

Coughing slightly, he continues. "Well, I certainly wasn't like Wendy at school. I was fanatic about doing the right thing." He drums his fingers on the table. "Homework in on time. Rule follower par excellence. Top of the class, of course. Not a single mistake. But it never seemed to add up to the great . . . get out of jail

204

204

free card I expected. I never felt right. Not later at college, not at home. So, I thought, I'll go back to Alcott. Yes, I'll be a teacher for a while, but then I'll sell my novel, be a success. But . . ."

"Didn't work," I say.

"No. Except"—his voice cracks—"for the girls. The girls were different. Prettier, sexier. And now they would talk to me. Even flirt with me. But now they were off-limits." He looks down at the hands in his lap. "Then when Wendy made it clear that she was . . . interested, I decided that for once, I wasn't going to . . ." He corrects himself. "I thought I—" He breaks off.

Finally he says, "I wanted to see what it felt like to do the wrong thing. Because doing the right thing . . ."

I think: being married, being a dad, being a teacher when you want to be a writer.

". . . didn't feel good." He sighs this last, stares down at the hands in his lap.

"So, what did wrong feel like?"

"Should I tell you awful?" He looks me in the eye. He's daring me to hear how wonderful Wendy was.

"Then what happened? If it was so great."

He looks down. "Nothing like that is great for long," he says in a low voice.

I think of that picture in his briefcase. The little boy with so much love.

Mr. Farrell continues. "You were right, Rain, when you said Wendy wasn't good at keeping secrets. When we started, she broke it off with Ellis. Said he was 'too nice a guy' to fool, and she didn't want to pretend. She expected me to not want to pretend too." He snorts slightly; I am meant to feel irritated with Wendy. How could she want what was so obviously impossible?

"That's when I realized, she was a girl who needed people to know she was loved—or what she thought was love."

He frowns. "People were starting to notice; Wendy was practically daring them to. So I said, If this is going to continue, you need to be more discreet. You have to keep the secret. And we need a cover, another guy. One who's not so nice."

"Nico."

He nods. I wait for signs that he's ashamed: a turn of the head, a cough, a fidget. Nothing. The fact that he framed one of his own students—with my help—doesn't seem to bother him.

I ask, "If Wendy didn't want to pretend, why'd she agree to it?"

"She didn't like it." Now he drops his head, clearly remembering arguments. "But Nico had treated her pretty badly over the summer. And she liked the idea of getting back at Sasha. Who, as you know, can be unkind." He gives a tight smile.

"Wendy seemed to really get into Nico, though."

"She did. I wondered at times," he says slowly, "if she was trying to make me jealous. Frankly, what I hoped was that she would move on to Nico, forget about me."

"But she didn't."

He shakes his head. "There started to be these . . . tests. Would I talk to her with other people around? Would I show her I cared? Prove it to her. One night I found my wife chatting with her on the phone. That was the wake-up call."

"So you told Wendy to get lost and she freaked."

"That about covers it," he says tensely.

"And you knew she was a girl who knew how to get back at people who hurt her, right? That the way she got back at people was by making a big noisy scene. To do something that would get everybody talking."

"She was going to tell my *wife*," he says. "Not to mention the school."

"Whose idea was it to meet in the park?"

"Mine."

"Were you already thinking . . ." My throat seizes up. I can barely think the words.

"No." He sits up, reaches out. "No, this was a terrible, terrible accident. Please. Please believe me about that. I never would have planned such a thing. I still . . ." He sits back, exhausted. "I still can't believe it happened."

He rubs his forehead. "I just wanted to talk to her. Somewhere no one would see us. Wendy had been saying, I want to see you, why can't I see you? And I was stupid enough to think that was all she wanted."

The bitterness creeps into his voice again, the blame.

"So I told her to meet me in the park that night. I said, Make sure you don't tell anyone you're going. If someone knows you're leaving the party, make sure they think it's about Nico."

"And Wendy did just what you told her."

"I thought we could have a rational conversation, that she would see that hurting my wife was wrong. I tried to explain to her that my wife would leave me, I would lose my job, that I would probably never see my son again. She didn't care. She wanted us together. Started saying that after she graduated, she would go to NYU, and we would *live* together."

It's so close to my fantasy, I flinch.

Farrell continues, "And when I said that couldn't be, she got so angry. She actually got out her cell phone . . ."

The one they never found, I think.

". . . and started dialing my home. 'Time to tell wifey,' she said. Nothing I said would make her stop. I begged her. I yelled at her. Finally, I had to physically—"

He breaks off, then says quietly, "Once I had . . . hurt her, I couldn't expect her not to tell people."

So you silenced her, choked the voice right out of her when you crushed her throat.

"What were you thinking?" I ask quietly. "When it was happening?"

He considers, wanting to get the answer right. "All I could think of, what kept going through my mind, was that the one time I do something wrong, I lose everything. It just seemed so unfair. The one *time*." His voice is almost whiny as he glares down at the table. He is not an adult. He's an angry boy.

"Do *you* think it's fair, Rain?" he asks softly. "For that one time, I have to . . ." He looks up, and for a moment, I feel sad for him.

Then he whispers, "I can be in the world, Rain. I can go back to being right. I was right with you. You . . . well, you liked me. I could have taken advantage of that. But I didn't. I did the right thing."

My spine goes ice. There's no air in my lungs. Behind my back, my hand searches for the doorknob.

Immediately, Farrell sees he's made a mistake. Raising his hand, he says, "Let's set that aside." He places his fingers on the table, drums them gently one after the other. "I know doing the right thing is very important to you. You're a good person." He looks up. "But you're also someone who understands that people with power are not always kind."

He searches my face, wanting to see if I'm buying it. I'm a freak, you're a freak. Don't hand me to the torturers.

I shake my head.

He nods quickly, as if he expected me to say no. "The thing is, Rain, even if you do . . . tell"—he smiles a little—"I'm not convinced that anyone will believe your story. As I said, much of the evidence does point toward Nico."

"Not all of it." I crack the door slightly. "There must be phone calls from Wendy to your house. Even if you got rid of her cell— there'll be a record. Talks you won't be able to explain away. Talks on the day she died."

"Oh, yes," he says calmly. "The police asked me about those. I explained that Wendy was having difficulties in my class, and I was trying to help her."

I say, "There were probably scratches, but of course nobody looked."

"No. No, they didn't."

An image in my head, Wendy's fingers clawing at Farrell's hands, the ones lying so casually on the table now.

To regain control, I focus on the facts, saying, "Even Wendy's Facebook name for the guy she was dating. She called him The Hot One. T.H.—your initials. And, of course, everything they knew about the E pin—the one piece of physical evidence—they learned from you." I cough. "One thing I don't get?"

"What?"

"Why didn't Dorland tell the police the pin wasn't from this year? That it couldn't possibly belong to a student now?"

"Oh." Farrell frowns. "Mr. Dorland was unable to meet with the police. He just didn't feel comfortable. And the bad publicity for the school has upset him very much. So I told him as acting head of school, I'd be happy to talk to the police, answer any questions they had."

"Why did you even tell them the school gave out pins?"

"I thought it was better to admit it rather than have them discover it from talking to the students. Of course, I stressed to them the great need for discretion. It would be best for their case and best for the students if they could keep the existence of the pin quiet until there was an actual arrest."

"But you had to know Nico didn't have one."

"Yes." He looks at me. "That's why when you came to me, told me about Sasha giving Nico the pin—well, I was grateful, to say the least."

"I'm sure. But just so you know, I've told Nico it wasn't Sasha's pin they found in the park. I told him to ask for a picture just to make sure. Oh—and I talked to Ms. Laredo, too. About how they changed the color and style of the pins over the years. So it probably won't be too long before the police figure out who the real owner of the E was."

"You've talked to a lot of people," he says slowly.

"Yes, I have."

For a moment, I see it through his eyes. We were supposed to be allies, setting Nico up, causing misery for Sasha, directing everyone's rage toward the rich, the beautiful, the entitled. I think of Mr. Farrell as a boy, wandering the halls of this school, watching, wanting, afraid to speak.

And hating.

"Do you understand?" His voice is weak, doubtful now.

I decide not to answer that, saying instead, "I think you know what I have to do."

A deep, deep sigh. Nodding, he turns his head, his eyes looking far, far away now. Past me. Past the door. In a ragged voice, as if someone's twisted a knife in his throat, leaving only the shreds of sinew, he says, "Yes, that's . . . you're right. I'm sorry, Rain. I'm . . ."

I can't stand to hear him say my name.

He's crying now. His shoulders are slumped, his legs skewed. The hands that killed Wendy frozen in front of his face, as if he wants to hide but can't bear to touch himself. The sobs are like blood, pumping out of a ruined heart.

Wendy is still dead. I hadn't understood before: it really doesn't bring them back. Somehow, you think, despite what you know, it will be a trade. Find the person who did the wrong thing and they will suffer instead of the one who was killed.

Instead, that person just suffers too.

But I suppose that's the best we can do.

I twist the doorknob, open the door. I half whisper "Good-bye" and walk out the door.

I am back in the crowd. Surrounded by voices. Faces spin by in a blur. I see Ms. Laredo coming down the hall. Seeing me, she stops. "Rain?"

S's have always kicked my ass. Also t's. That makes *Mister* a word I avoid. It comes out *Mithder*.

People are slowing down around me. Stopping. Staring. I open my mouth. Think: I can't.

Go for it, tigress.

And I say it.

"Mr. Farrell killed Wendy Geller."

AFTER

"Are you ready?"

On the last day of school, Alcott says farewell to its seniors and welcome to its new senior class. Each senior and junior carries a candle. The seniors' candles are lit; ours are not. When your name is called, you walk onstage and a senior lights your candle from hers. Then the seniors leave the stage and the new senior class is presented to the school. Being a senior at Alcott, Mr. Dorland tells us, means something. We represent the sum of an Alcott education; the high values and intellectual achievement Alcott imparts to its graduates. Or, as Taylor says, what $35,000 a year buys.

But I can't feel cynical today. For one thing, I've learned I'm not as cynical as I thought I was. I am going to miss a lot of these people. Ellis, who's headed to Cornell. Lindsey, who's off to Stanford. Rima, who is going to Carleton. And while I won't miss Nico Phelps, I'll certainly never forget him.

Nico is not here today. After Mr. Farrell pled guilty to murdering Wendy, the school let Nico quietly finish out the year, mostly working from home. He and Sasha broke up. I heard he did apply to Brown but didn't get in. He's probably not that disappointed; he has a book contract for half a million to write about the Wendy Geller murder. The book will be called *Falsely Accused*.

I have seen him, of course—along with the rest of the country—when he did that interview on CNN. They asked me if I wanted to be on the show. I said no thanks. Which is what I've said to everyone who's wanted my "side of the story." I have told exactly two people everything that happened: my mother and Taylor.

It was hard, telling my mother. Because I told her the whole story about Mr. Farrell, how I felt about him, all of it. We sat on the couch, me wrapped up in her arms, my face pressed against her body, and we cried. For Wendy, for me, for two girls who weren't such "very different girls" after all.

Then my mom said, almost as a joke, "Hey, maybe someday we should have a talk about your father."

I laughed. "There's a messy situation."

She sighed. "Human connection—very messy. Unpredictable." Then she went all operatic: "Entirely too dangerous!"

Connections. Wendy to Nico. Wendy to Mr. Farrell. Mr. Farrell to me. Me to Wendy. Nico to Sasha. Ellis, Lindsey. All this emotion, all this hurt and want. So much that somebody died.

Now, waiting in the wings, I see Mr. Dorland sitting in the front row. This is his final senior class. He'll be retiring at the end of the year. Ms. Johnson will fill in when she comes back from maternity leave. I hope they give her the job permanently. Alcott needs to make some changes.

They call Taylor's name, and she goes up to be greeted by Bradley Tournival, her coeditor on the paper. This gets a huge roar of approval from the crowd. Part of the fun of this ceremony is seeing who is matched with who; since Taylor is taking over from Bradley and they're friends, this is a good match. Seniors can request, or the school puts pairs together. I can see that even Taylor is struggling to keep it together as Bradley gives her a kiss. I swear I see her wipe away a tear.

Cantor, Christie, Danilowicz . . . finally they call my name. Rain Donovan. As I start to walk down the aisle, I wonder who I'll get. Kids like me usually get the light from one of the official "nice kids," school officers who understand it's part of their job to make sure everyone has a match.

But when Sasha walks out onto the stage, my face burns and tears come to my eyes. Surprise, happiness, humility, guilt . . . I feel it all at the same mind-blowing instant. Sasha has been out much of this semester; when she's been in school, she's kept to herself. We have not talked, and I suspect that's because neither of us has known what the hell to say.

Now she stands there calmly as I approach, candle held in both hands. The applause is tentative at first; people aren't sure what to think. Everyone remembers that Sasha dated Nico, that I was the one who proved Nico wasn't guilty—and that Sasha clobbered me in the hall that time. But slowly, the applause starts to grow louder.

I manage a goofy grin as Sasha touches her light to mine, but there are tears rolling down my face. Sasha kisses me on both cheeks. First cheek, she whispers, "I'm sorry." The second, "Thank you."

The rest of the names go by in a blur. As Queenie Richardson lights Jenny Zalgat's candle and leaves the stage, the rest of us turn to face the school as the new senior class. I am standing in the first row. Jenny comes to stand near me. Between us is an empty seat. On it is an unlit candle. And a photograph of Wendy.

Together we say, "In memory of our friend, Wendy Geller."

A month ago, a group of us got together to talk about how we wanted to remember Wendy at the ceremony. At the time, we weren't sure whether to light the candle or not. I thought not was more honest. Wendy doesn't get to carry her flame forward. Mr. Farrell put it out.

That's how it was going to be until Jenny spoke up suddenly. "Yeah, but, okay, so she isn't here, like her 'light' is not here, whatever, but I feel like she kind of gave it to us, you know? She definitely had an effect on my life. She was the first person to tell me I wasn't an idiot." She ducked her head. "She said I had a genius heart." She smiled.

Ellis smiled. "She said I had way cool fashion sense. Geek chic."

Daniel Ettinger said, "She said zits were a sign of high testosterone and masculinity."

Everyone cracked up. In the laughter, a thousand Wendys flashed through my mind.

Speak up, girl!

Do I know you?

The dough rocks raw.

She should know to say hi.

Hey there!

There is no one Wendy, I realized. Her mom's sweet, funny little baby; the chick who boasted about getting trashed on Facebook. The girl who was such a good friend to people, the bitch who trampled others' feelings because she was blinded by her own hurt. All those things are true, but no one thing is the whole truth.

I saw Jenny looking at me. What was my vote? Does Wendy have a light or no?

I said, "Let's go for it, tigress."

Jenny smiled. "Cool—but only if you sing. Wendy always said you had a kick-ass voice."

Now as I walk to the front of the stage, I feel my heart beating so hard, I can't catch my breath. To calm down, I think of something else—anything but the hundreds of eyes on me right now, the ears all listening.

Wendy, I realize. I should think of Wendy.

For a moment, Mr. Farrell creeps into my head. A twist in my stomach, sour in my throat. I still have nightmares, in which I am the girl being strangled because I asked for too much. In these dreams, I scream, my throat muscles strain, but there is no sound. Just Mr. Farrell's hands and the crushing weight.

Some nights when I wake up, I think, I wish I'd never gone through that door. That first day of school after Wendy was killed. I wish I'd never talked to him. Because I still feel guilty. Wendy wasn't the only person blinded by her own hurt. Who was unkind to others out of that hurt. Am I smarter now?

But if I had not gone through that door, Nico Phelps would probably be in jail and Mr. Farrell would not be. And I would still think you can get through life safe and sound and pure— and actually have a life. I wouldn't know the only way not to make a mistake is never to do anything at all.

In which case, says Wendy's voice, you might as well be in a box like me. Now, can you please sing, already? I've been waiting a long time.

We had a lot of discussion about which song would be right for Wendy. Sarah McLachlan's "I Will Remember You" is beautiful, but a lot of people do it. I thought "Into the West" from *Lord of the Rings*, because it's tender and sad, about journeys' ends.

But it was too proper for Wendy somehow. And I'm not Annie Lennox.

Finally, my mom, of all people, came up with "Yesterday's Child" by Patti Scialfa. The second I heard the lines "And I still have my imaginings/Where there's no struggling/Or suffering/Just cigarettes and wine," I knew it was the right song for Wendy.

Singing in the chorus, I have always wondered what it would be like to stand alone, to have only your voice heard. How terrifying it would be to know it was all up to you. And how you'd have to keep going, even if you screwed up big-time.

But what I could not imagine was the incredible rush when you connect. When you feel the audience. All they want to hear is your voice, because it lets them feel what they need to.

My voice does crack a few times, where the feelings get too big. But it doesn't matter. I sing the last verse, reminding myself that Wendy would want this to be joyous, defiant.

> SO LET'S RAISE THE GLASS
> TO A SYMPHONY OF MILES
> AND SAY OUR LAST FAREWELL
> TO YESTERDAY'S CHILD.

As I finish and the applause starts, I don't want to say farewell to Wendy. But I have to. She's gone. And with her, a scared little girl who never said what she thought or felt. I'll miss that girl, too. Even though I'm glad not to be her anymore.

Who knows? Maybe in some alternate universe, she and Wendy are sitting and eating cookie dough. And laughing.